PRINCE OF TIGERS BOOK 4

KATHI S. BARTON

World Castle Publishing, LLC
Pensacola, Florida
Copyright © Kathi S. Barton 2021
Paperback ISBN: 9781953271709
eBook ISBN: 9781953271716
First Edition World Castle Publishing, LLC, February 8, 2021
http://www.worldcastlepublishing.com

Cover: Karen Fuller
Editor: Maxine Bringenberg

Prologue

Kylan was running behind, as usual. He had been at his apartment cleaning out his fridge when he was told they were having dinner together tonight. Just as he was finishing his clean up, Summer came to speak to him.

"Your house is complete, sir." He looked at Summer and asked her what she was talking about. "Your mate. I've been to see her, and she has wonderful ideas about your home you'll share with her. I'd not be surprised if she were to fall in love with you this night."

"I don't have a mate, Summer." She smiled at him. "How do you know what my mate wants in a house when I don't know a thing about her? In addition to that, what do you mean, she'll fall in love with me this night? I don't have any plans to leave the house."

"She is coming with her family for dinner tonight. Lady Piper spoke with her just today." Kylan asked her what that had to do with him. "Why everything, my lord. You'll be so happy with her daughter as well. Your mate's daddy, he is most ill, but we can fix him up when he is ready."

Kylan sat down and thought about what she was telling him. "What's her name?" Summer asked him if he meant her daughter or his mate. "Both. For that matter, who told you she was my mate?"

"I know these things. But it was Lady Piper that told me about her. She is so very beautiful, sir. Her hair is like the sunshine, it is so bright. Her daughter has dark hair like yours. Also, your mate—her name is Emmaline, but her dad calls her Emmie—has one blue eye and one green eye. She covers it with contacts, but even without them showing, she is very lovely. A perfect match for you."

Now he was headed to Fisher's home for dinner and to meet his mate. The big rig in the drive of their home was the first indication of what she did for a living. Going to the back door, not wanting to be pushed into something that was wrong, he saw Piper there waiting on him. She looked too slick for his tastes.

"Summer told you, didn't she?" He asked Piper if it was true. "It is. She's very outspoken but nice when it suits her." She told him about the man who was now working for her.

"How are you finding this out, Piper? Did you get some sort of vision magic that you've not told anyone about?" She grinned and told him she had. "Is she going to be happy to find out I'm her mate? Or are we going to have a battle on our hands? Is her family going to come around and beat me up too?"

"The only family she has is her father and daughter. The father of her daughter, Olivia, is dead, killed by his father when he raped Emmie when she was only fourteen years old." Kylan sat down at the kitchen table, waiting for the next part of Piper's tale. He knew there was more to it than she was saying, but he didn't ask. "There is no one chasing them—no bad people after them. They're not wealthy like you are, but they have learned to stretch a dollar until it screams, as her dad says. There isn't a bad skeleton in their closet that they're going to keep from anyone. Collier, her father, is a recovering drunk but has been sober for nearly eighteen years. They're just a family that has had some bad things happen to them, but they've recovered nicely."

"Who else knows she's my mate other than the three of us?" She told him she'd not even told Fisher yet. "What's going on here, Piper? I don't know why, but I have a feeling things aren't as cut and dried as you've made them out to be."

"She's an attorney. A damned good one too." Nodding, he told her he and his brothers had been attorneys several times over their lives. "Emmie specializes in corporate law. Like I said, she's damned good at it too. We need her in this family as much as you're going to need her as your mate."

"I don't understand this." She told him that was all right. He would. "You've told me I have a mate, then leave me hanging about why she's so important to this family. That's not very sisterly of you."

"No, I suppose it's not. What if I told you she needs to be a part of this family so you can save her father's life? Make him have a good feeling about himself." Kylan told her he could do that without taking a mate. "Why are you being so obtuse about this? I'm trying to do the right thing here and not give you too much information before you've met."

"Is that important?" Piper nodded. "All right. I'll not ask you anymore about her. But I do have to know, why is it that you've told me this? I can understand you've got rules about not telling too much of what the future holds, but you've told me a great deal."

When her house phone rang, she told him it was for him. Going to the phone, he picked it up and said his name. He heard the words being said to him, but he was having a difficult time making them into information after the first comment. After telling the officer where he was and how long he'd been there, he hung up the phone.

"My apartment complex blew up forty minutes ago." She didn't say anything but did hand him a glass of water. "Everything is gone. No one was home, so they're all safe. You knew this. Didn't you?"

"When I saw what happened, I knew I had to get

you from the house. You would have been there had I only invited you to dinner. You would have come here, but it would have been too late for you to get out. So I told you of your mate so you'd leave early enough not to be there when the boiler burst." He nodded. "It was the only way, Kylan. I didn't know what else to do. I can't see you hurt."

"Thank you." He thought about what she'd said to him. "You said I have to save her father's life. Was that it? Did he come to my apartment too?"

"No. He needs you in another way."

Getting up, he staggered a little but made his way to the living room. He saw Olivia first. If she looked only half like her mom, he was going to be in deep trouble with the beautiful women to come into his life.

Kylan hugged his mom and dad, introduced himself to Collier, and sat down on the couch where his brothers were. He looked at Emmie as she spoke to Harper about the runs she'd taken out for them today. When Emmie looked at him, Kylan knew he'd been wrong. He was going to be in more than just trouble with his new mate. He was going to be running around with his tongue hanging out whenever he saw her. Christ, she was more than beautiful. She was gorgeous.

The poke to his ribs had him looking at his mom. "You're staring at her like you're going to eat her alive. If you keep that up, young man, she's going to hurt you." He looked at his mom. "I've only just met her, but I have a feeling she won't hold back if you do something to cause her trouble. Is she your mate?"

"Yes." Mom nodded and leaned back on the couch, pulling him back with her. "She's beautiful, isn't she? I mean, all women are beautiful, but she's...she's beyond that."

"What the hell is wrong with you?" He looked back at the woman they'd been speaking of. "You're staring at me like I'm some sort of shit under your foot. Either say what you have to say or stop looking at me like that."

"You're my mate." There was a deafening silence in the room. "I only just found out myself. You're very beautiful."

When Emmie stood up, he did as well. Not only was she good looking, but she was also nearly as tall as he was. He'd estimate she was at least six feet, if not a little more. Before he could pull her to him, if he had that thought in his head, Olivia stood between them. She was shooting daggers at him with her eyes.

"Hello." Olivia didn't so much as utter a single word to him. "I'm Kylan Prince. You must be her daughter."

"I'm the spitting image of my mother. If you don't back off right now, mister, I don't know people's space bubble—I'm gonna hurt you. I've been trained by the best there is in defending myself and others." He smiled at her and told Olivia he was glad to know that. "You won't be if you're picking up your nuts from across the room."

"Now, see here." Mom got up and came to stand by him and his new family members. "You might be able to speak that way at home, young lady, but you will hold your tongue on —"

"She's not allowed to speak like that anywhere." Emmie told Olivia to apologize to Mrs. Prince. When she did, Olivia also told her that her mother raised her better than that. "I'm going to keep right on raising her better than you did this moron. Not that I'm blaming you. I guess not everyone takes to being a good person like the rest of your family apparently has."

"Kylan does have his days. How about we all have a seat, then we can see what there is to know about the rest of you." Alarm ran over his body when he heard one of his brothers calling to Collier. Moving toward the man, he could see that not only were his eyes glazed over in apparent pain, but his lips were blue. Kylan heard his mother speak as he was helping Collier to the floor. "Call an ambulance. Be quick about it."

Taking off the tie he had on, Kylan spoke to the elder man. He told him what he was doing with each step that he took. Emmie was on the other side of her dad, telling him to open his mouth. Before he could do what she wanted, his eyes closed, and Kylan knew the man was going to need more than just his help, but everyone's.

Performing CPR, he didn't stop until Emmie said

it was her turn. Before the ambulance arrived, two of his brothers had helped with the rotation. Not that he couldn't have done it for a lot longer, but he didn't want to mess up by hurting her father while he was trying to save him.

The EMTs came in with their equipment and switched off with him when they had his chest exposed. It only took them seconds to hit him with the defibrillator and bring the man back. They were hooking Collier up to an IV and calling in his vitals when Olivia came and hugged him.

"He's my grandda. And besides my mom, all I have in the world. You saved him for me." Holding her as he stood up, he wasn't the least bit surprised to see Emmie sitting on the couch now with her head between her knees. "Can you talk to my mom? Don't touch her. She'll scream if you do. Just talk to her and not touch her."

Kylan didn't understand the no touching part, but he did sit on the couch with Emmie and spoke to her. He wasn't telling her anything substantial, but just telling her what the EMTs were doing as they worked to keep her father alive. When Emmie sat up, he asked her if she was all right.

"I should have noticed he wasn't well." Kylan said those closest to people sometimes didn't see things. He was guilty of the same thing. "Don't pamper me with niceties. I should have noticed he wasn't feeling well when we drove here today. He said his head hurt and that his belly was upset. If you think you might have even the slightest chance of making me your mate, you'll never lie to me or try and sugarcoat things that are going on. I won't have it."

"All right. I had a little bit of a warning when I got here that he might need me. I was on top of it because of that." She asked him if it had been Piper. "It was. She and my brother work for some very powerful people, the queen of the earth, Aurora, and she gifted them with all kinds of magic. That's me not sugarcoating things. Why did your daughter tell me not to touch you?"

"I've been raped before, and sometimes I have trouble with sudden moves and touches. What did she tell you about us?" He told her about the explosion and the reason he was told about her. "So you only know I'm your mate because someone told you I was. Is that the way it works?"

"No. I can smell you. Your scent calls to me. It also warns other males, other cats, that you're a mate to someone powerful." She asked him what that meant. "I'm a very old and very powerful tiger. Black tiger, as a matter of fact."

"I won't give up my daughter without a fight. And I'm including death to you if you even try." He said he'd never ever do that to her or to Olivia. "We'll see. I have to go to the hospital. My dad is going to need me. He's on all kinds of antidepressants."

"May I go? The hospital might need me to answer some questions about what happened." She told him to suit himself. "Will Olivia want to go?"

"I'm not leaving her alone with strangers." But in the end, Olivia wanted to stay. Kylan knew it was costing Emmie to leave her only child there, but Olivia said she'd be fine and was stressed out too much to wait on someone to tell them what was going on. "All right. But you know the rules and what to do."

"I do, Mom. I'll be fine."

His mom didn't say anything, but he could tell she was curious. He was as well, but he didn't ask either of them what the rules were. Instead, he got his car so that Emmie could ride with him to the hospital. He had a feeling it was going to be a long night. Kylan only hoped it was going to be a good night rather than snipping at him like she had been doing.

Although, he was enjoying her show of temper.

Chapter 1

Kylan thought of the things, little hints, that he'd gotten from Emmie. She'd been raped before. While he didn't have any details on when or how that had happened, he figured Olivia was the product of it. He reached out to Allie and asked her what she knew of a rape that happened fifteen years ago.

I have it right here. I was looking it up right after I got home. Olivia is at Samson's house. She and his daughters are watching television. She's a mouthy little thing. Not to mention sharp. There is no pulling the wool over her eyes. Kylan asked her if she'd said anything more to his mom. *No. To be honest, Kylan, she's not said a great deal of anything. I was referring to what she said to you. Even asking her questions directly doesn't get us much in the way of information about her. Let's see. Here it is. It was three days before Emmie's fourteenth birthday when she was taken. Apparently, she knocked around one of the kidnappers enough that the little guy he was working on getting into his van was able to get away. She wasn't so lucky. The son, a big hulking guy, hit her from behind, or she might well have gotten away too. The article goes on to say that the son, Herbie Landry, not the father, Herbert, raped her brutally.* He asked her what had happened after that. *Herbert beat the shit out of her for the three days he had her, for her spoiling him getting his prize. It was assumed by Emmie that he meant the little boy that had gotten away. However, he never touched her sexually. With her nearly starved and tied up, the son came home when the dad was out and raped her. Dad caught him at it, and while she was getting away, they killed each other. She's lucky she wasn't killed, too, from the way the article reads.*

So at fourteen, she had a baby. That must have been hard on both of them. Allie told him it was worse than that. *Tell me. I don't want to go over her head for answers, but I have a feeling this will be the only way I get information. She is as tight lipped as the daughter.*

When she was home, her dad made arrangements to get the homework that she'd missed. The school board decided they didn't want her to come back to school. Something about her being a terrible thing to see for the other students. Then when they found out about the baby, she had to finish her education online — poor kid. I wish I had known her then. I would have raised holy hell for her. Kylan pointed out that she could still do it. *Nah. I think Emmie can hold her own on most things. Also, before I forget to tell you the rules. I'm sure you heard that there were rules Olivia has to follow. They're scary rules, Kylan. She can't find herself alone with strangers, or she is to run. No eating anything she's not seen prepared. And if that isn't possible, she is to take food from the bottom of the serving platter so she'll not be subject to whatever kinds of poisons may have been put in it. What sort of person teaches their child to be so wary of others?*

A person who has an alcoholic father and has been raped by a monster. Allie said there was that. *I'm going to stay here for as long as she'll let me. I guess I have a house now. Summer told me it was finished, as she knew what Emmie wanted in the house. Hang on, Allie. The doctor is coming toward us.*

"Ms. Rankin, I've admitted your dad. He's suffering badly from anxiety and depression. He is also having some issues with his liver that I'm assuming are from drinking heavily." Emmie told the doctor he'd been sober for nearly eighteen years. "That's more than likely the only reason he's around today. You should know that I might have to keep him here for a few days until he's a little stronger. I'd like to have him see someone while he's here, and that might take a few days. Thank you for telling the staff about what he is taking daily. I've spoken to your dad as well. He's very upset that he has embarrassed you and that he's hurt you and Olivia. Is that his wife?"

"No. His granddaughter. They're very close. She can sit with him, and he'll calm down most of the time. But lately, I don't think even that is working." He said he could tell that. "Dad hasn't had a good life. I've tried my best to keep him safe, but it's beginning to drain me. Will you be upping his medications?"

"Have a seat." She sat down in the chair behind her, and since she didn't tell Kylan to leave, he sat too. When she took his hand into her own, Kylan had a feeling she knew whatever the doctor was going to say was going to be earthshattering for her little family. "I'm not sure your father can cope in the world anymore, Ms. Rankin. You've done a remarkable job thus far, but hearing him talking and knowing what sort of medications he's on, I think it would be better if he were someplace that would keep him on his meds and make sure he's safe."

"Are you telling me he's not safe with me?" Dr. Franklin told her he wasn't. "I see. And you've figured this out by having a conversation with him and knowing what his medications are. Meds that he takes daily because I'm there to make sure he does. What sort of condition have you fabricated that makes you think my dad isn't safe? What the fuck is your reasoning behind saying something like that to me?"

Dr. Franklin looked to Kylan, and Kylan laughed. "If you think I'm going to step in and save your ass, you're stupider than I thought when you came up with this hairbrained idea that that man in there isn't safe. I've only known Emmie and her daughter for a short time, but I can tell you right now that no one on this earth is more devoted or able to care for him or keep him safe as the two of them. Was he hurt anywhere? Did he have some sort of bruising that can't be explained?" Dr. Franklin said other than the bruising on his chest, no. "So, this safety thing, you're just pulling it out of your ass. Even I understand you're supposed to do a thorough observation on someone before you jump to the conclusion that he needs to be put away. That's what you're talking about, isn't it? And don't you dare fob me off or lie to me about it."

"I get a kickback on sending people like him that won't be any trouble to the home once they're highly medicated. They get the care they need when it's necessary, and the family is free to have a little fun. It doesn't hurt anyone." Kylan asked him how many times he'd done this in his career. "Hundreds. It's good for me. I'm able to afford all the luxuries I thought would come with being a doctor. How the hell was I supposed to figure out that I'd have to work twice as hard as anyone else and that I'd be puked on? I fucking hate when that happens."

Kylan looked at Emmie. "What do you want to do?" She looked at him as if she'd never seen him before. "I told you I was a black tiger and had magic. I only made him tell us the truth because I no more believed you weren't taking good care of him than you did. I'm going to contact the police, then I'm going to contact my family. You tell me what it is you want, and I'll get it for you."

"I want him evaluated. Properly." He reached out

to Allie, but Emmie touched her hand to his shoulder first. "Is there a way to find out which nursing home he's getting the kickback from? The mother fucker is ruining lives, and I, for one, would like to make the nursing home pay too."

After telling his entire family what they'd encountered, Allie told him she was going to do some digging, as well as Piper and the others. Dad and Mom said they'd be there soon with Olivia and that they'd bring dinner.

By the time his family all came in force, he not only knew the name of the nursing home but who it was the doctor was getting the money from. It was the management, not the staff, which saved them from having to fire the entire staff for what they were doing.

Kylan was careful not to just take over on this. Emmie was with him every step of the way and had suggestions for everything they were doing. If he wasn't impressed with her before, he certainly was now. Not only did she know the laws governing such moves as the one Franklin was doing, but she also knew the fines, as well as the sentencing Franklin would get when convicted. And he would be, Kylan would see to that.

By the time several doctors had been called to come in and have a look at Collier, he was awake again and wanting his daughter. Emmie sat with him for over an hour while the doctors asked him questions, gave him an exam, and looked over the medication he'd been taking. It wasn't until Dr. Franklin was taken to jail that Dr. Kirby came to talk to him and Emmie. His parents had asked if they could be there as well, as they wanted to help. They were sitting at a long table while Olivia sat with her new grandda.

"It's small wonder he's been able to function at all, Ms. Rankin. Three of the medications he was taking were giving him heart palpitations. That is what caused him to nearly die at the Prince's home. Also, I will tell you if not for the quick work that was done when he did stop breathing, we'd be talking about something entirely different. In addition to those three drugs, another one of them was making him hallucinate. Badly. With all that going on inside of his mind and body, it's a salute to you and your daughter that you were able to keep him alive. You should be commended for your help with him."

"He's my dad." Dr. Kirby told her she was a good daughter. "What can we do now? I mean, the other idiot wanted to shove him into a nursing home."

"I see no reason, now that he's taking a good regimen, that he can't function at home or with you. I would like to keep him in here for a few days, just to make sure he has no side effects from the change in his medication." She said to do whatever was needed to make him better. "Oh, he will be. You should notice a difference in his health right away. As for his liver, while it is in somewhat of a bad shape, he's been sober long enough that it's healing nicely as well. I would suggest you have him eat better foods. What I mean is, he should be eating more fruits and vegetables. He told me when I spoke to him that he's more of a meat and potato man. I told him he needed to broaden his food intake."

"I will." Kylan had no doubt that before they got back to his parents' home, she'd have a list of food to get for him. "Will this medication change make him feel better about himself? He's had some hard blows hit him, and I'd like for him to be less paranoid than he is now."

"This medication will calm him a great deal. In doing so, he'll be able to think things through better, so he's not overwhelmed all the time. This will be something he'll need to work on. Telling him to stop and think about what has him so excited might be a good way to remind him that he's better. I will tell you, Ms. Rankin, that he's worried so much about you and your daughter. I don't want you to stop talking to him. In fact, just the opposite. Tell him what is going on, so he doesn't think up things when he knows you're stressed too. If you're in a bad mood, tell him what happened, so his mind doesn't make up things that are worse than they are."

Dad laughed. "I don't think she will have any trouble keeping her daddy informed. She certainly didn't us." Dad patted Emmie on the hand and smiled at her. "You've done a good job, honey—a very good job. You should be proud of yourself. And I know there are a lot of people out there that are going to benefit from you taking a stand with that other fool. You did good."

Things were going on around the hospital that he was only just being made aware of. The doctor, of course, had been fired, along with some staff members. Collier was getting the best of care, it seemed, mostly due to Emmie not taking any shit. But his name held a lot of power as well.

Mom told him it had been going on for some time, this putting people away so the government would pay the nursing home for caring for people like Emmie's dad. All they did was dope them up and then ignore them until they had to help them.

"I hate to think of someone's loved ones being treated that way." Emmie told his mom she wouldn't have stood for it. "No, you wouldn't have. I can see that about you. You would have been there daily, ensuring he was getting the care he should have been getting. Yes, that's wonderful of you. But there are others out there that would just as soon put their family members away, so they don't have to mess with them. It's not a very good way to treat someone that brought you into this world."

Dr. Kirby told them that Emmie could go and see her dad when she was ready. But he did make them aware that he was a little doped up, simply because the medication he'd been given before him getting his case was doing that. Emmie took Kylan's hand into hers again, and they went to the room. Her dad did look a good deal better, simply because he was no longer fretting about things.

When he smiled at him, Kylan took his hand when it was offered. "You saved my life, young man." He said it was a family effort. "Might have been, but from where I'm lying, you did it. Olivia here tells me that you and Emmie are mates. You couldn't do any better than my little girl."

"Dad, how are you feeling?" He told her what the doctor had said. That Dr. Kirby had been taking very good care of him. "They're going to keep you for a few days, he said. To make sure you're not going to have any more reactions to the medications he's put you on."

"I did tell that other man I wasn't sure I was taking the right drugs. He told me he was the doctor and I should just shut up. I've not been spoken to that way in a long time. But I didn't talk anymore." He looked at him. "Son, I'm ever so grateful for you being there for my girls. Knowing you're going to be watching over them for me means I can get myself gathered up and better. I want to now. I know now that all those things that were going on with me, they weren't my fault. You've no idea how much better that's made me feel already."

"It's my pleasure, sir. And when you're out of here, you and the girls have a place to stay. Until Emmie and I have had a chance to talk things over, she's going to be staying at the house I have. I'll be bunking with my parents for a little while." Collier just looked at his daughter, then smiled at him. "It's all right. I've got a feeling my family is going to offer Emmie a job too."

"I didn't say I'd take it." He knew better than to talk to her about it now. She was tensed up again. "I'll talk to them when I get back. I don't know where we're going to be staying, but you can count on me being here every day, Dad. I promise you that."

When they left the hospital, Olivia said she was hungry. Stopping at a fast-food restaurant wasn't what he'd like for them to be doing on their first outing, but it wasn't so bad. Olivia had a salad while he and Emmie had burgers and fries. It was going to take them both awhile to get used to him being there for them, Kylan thought. But he could wait. He had forever to wait for them.

~*~

Olivia wasn't sure what she was supposed to be feeling right now. Her heart was mixed up about all kinds of things. Was she supposed to like the Prince family? Because she did sort of like them. Was she okay with Kylan being her mom's mate? She knew what the word meant, but not so much with her mom. Her mom, her grandda told her, was hard on men. When Kylan entered the kitchen with her, she asked him if he wanted breakfast.

"I wouldn't mind having whatever you're having." Olivia had also discovered the refrigerator was magical. Whatever she wanted, it was just simply there. Putting a glass in front of him, she wasn't surprised when it filled itself with orange juice. "Are you all right living here with me here too?"

"That would be my mom's decision on where you live, I think. But I do love this house." Olivia put on a few slices of bacon for Kylan, thinking about the weird things she'd noticed about this place. "You have a pool now. I mean, it might well have been something I dreamed up, but Mom likes to swim too. If you want it gone, I'd understand."

"I like to swim as well. If you want something, be sure to make it known to either Summer, my faerie, or Pudge. He's your mom's faerie, but he'll help you as well. At least until we get you one of your own." She turned and looked at him. "You didn't think you'd be going without one, did you?"

Summer sat on the table in front of the plate she'd put on there for Kylan. While she didn't talk much, Pudge seemed to never shut up. But she loved the little guy. Turning over the bacon, she asked Kylan what they were going to do now.

"I'm not sure what you mean. You tell me, and I'll see if I can answer you. However, if you're asking me to do something for you, I won't do that without your mom knowing about it." She said she knew that. "Good. What did you need?"

"There is a pretty park like place at the back of this house." She turned around, then sat in the chair across from him to explain. "I've been homeschooled since I was a little girl. I don't fit in well with other children, the same as my mom didn't when she was younger. Too smart."

"That's wonderful. What do you want at the back of the house, Olivia? I'm game for just about anything you'd need. I'm assuming this has something to do with your education." She nodded. "All right. Summer here can help you with whatever you need. However, it would be nice if I knew what that might be."

"I want a place to work from. Not an office or anything like that, but I'd like to take my online classes in a smallish building. Pudge told me he can fix it up for me so I can have Internet as well as a safe place. I used to have an area at home on the back porch that I used as my own space. But grandda would visit me, and I'd be distracted. Not that I don't love him — I very much do — but I need a quiet place to work. If you don't mind." Kylan asked her if she studied better when she had her own space. "I do. Looking out over the yard isn't a distraction for me. It's hearing the household — phones ringing, pans banging around — that does that. I just need a small place I can call my own. For studying."

"My lady, I can fix that up for you." Summer looked at Kylan, then back at her. "But if you'd not mind, I'd like to introduce you to your faerie. I know you are a brilliant young woman, so we have paired you with an older faerie so you can learn from his wisdom. Cart is very nice, but he is very magical as well."

"I'm not sure what I can learn from him that won't

be on the computer for me, but I'll love having him around." Summer told her what she meant. "Oh. That's better. Yes, I'd love to learn from him about magic and the way things are done around here. I nearly screamed when I got down a glass, and it filled on its own."

"You'll notice a great many things now you're in this house that you might not have seen where you lived before. I would also like to remind you that when you are in the yard, or even at one of my brothers', there might be tigers around. I understand you've seen them in zoos, but you should be aware that my brother Fisher and his wife Allie are much larger even than Bryant. They work for Aurora."

"She came to talk to me yesterday while I was at your brother's house." She filled his plate with eggs, bacon, and fried potatoes. Hers was the same, but with much smaller portions and no bacon. "She told me I have magic too. But because of my only being fourteen, she's not given me any more than she thought I can handle. I don't know what I can handle, to be honest with you, Kylan, but it's fun being able to have whatever I want to wear."

"I bet it is. I especially like it when I'm out and about and don't have any extra clothing when I've had to shift. It's very hard on clothing when I have to do it quickly." She nodded at him and played with her food. "Whatever is bothering you, Olivia, if you don't want to talk to me about it, I'm sure there are any number of people around that will listen."

She wanted to just blurt it out, to tell him what she was worried about, but she wasn't sure whether he'd think she was being selfish. Looking up at the tall man, she was both relieved and sad when her mom joined them. Olivia gave Mom her plate of food and got up to make herself one.

"Olivia, have you figured out what you want to do around here yet?" Kylan didn't ask what they were talking about but ate his breakfast. "Also, I want you to give a little thought to what we spoke about last night. About the pack school that Sara was telling us about."

"I want to homeschool." She did too. Other children didn't like her. Olivia knew it was because she was so awkward around children her own age, but being in a classroom setting might just be too much for her. "I was just asking Kylan if I could have my own space at the back of the yard. Where I can go and not be bothered."

"Before we get too much further into the homeschooling, did my mom mention that the pack has a gifted program? There are only ten kids in the class, but they're brilliant like you are. Well ahead in the way of education too. You can go there anytime you wish to check it out. Either way you want to finish your education is going to be fine with me." Mom asked Kylan what sort of classes they had. "I think it depends on what the student wants to learn. I know there is a kid named Patrick that goes there. He takes a lot of online college courses while he learns the things for his passion at the school. They have other people come in too, depending on what your interests are, to help guide you in the things you will need to know. Patrick is studying marine biology. His idea is that he wishes to work with an oceanic company that knows how to save sea creatures before they're all gone."

"Mom, can I go? Just to check that out?" Mom told her she could so long as she went with her. "Okay. That way, if you have any questions about fees or anything, you can know it right away. Thanks, Kylan."

He nodded his answer to her and went back to his breakfast. Olivia didn't usually get excited about much. She'd never been a kid that was jumping in and out of things without careful thought to it. Her mom had taught her that. Wasting time jumping around would make it so that you didn't know what you were into. She liked her mother's approach to things. Well, most of the time.

As she was cleaning up her breakfast, Kylan told her he'd do the dishes since she'd cooked. Olivia had come to the conclusion that Kylan wasn't putting on an act for them, but he was genuinely a nice guy. But then, like a lot of things she'd learned, time would tell.

Summer asked her if she'd go into the living room with her to meet Cart. The little man was just what she thought Santa would have looked like—a long white beard, fuzzy hair, and he actually had on pointy shoes. When Olivia sat down, he came to stand on her knee. He bowed to her and then sat.

"I'm thinking you and I are going to find us some fun. What do you think?" Olivia said she wasn't really good at fun. "Oh, I think you've just been a waiting on the right faerie to come along and show you how to have it. Today I thought the two of us would get to know each other, then we can go out to the gardens. I can show you all kinds of things there that you won't believe."

After getting permission from her mom to go into the yard, Cart showed her where she could be with all manner of faeries and brownies. Not knowing the difference, she sat down on the little cushion he'd made for her and watched as he pointed out what they were doing today.

"You see the little fella carrying the bucket? He's a brownie. There isn't much in the way of telling the difference from here, but when you see him up close, you'll see it." Cart called for Apple, the little man with the bucket. She could see right away how the two men were different. "You see there, his wings? They're not as big as mine, as he only has to fly from flower to flower to get the nectar. I might have to travel great long distances to be with you. Also, Pick will be very helpful in keeping old seeds in check. There isn't a person around that can tell when a seed needs to have a rest better than a brownie. It's why they're so very helpful in the garden."

Olivia was happy Cart told her how helpful all the creatures they met today were to the colony. Not only was Pick good at making sure the nectar was ready to be taken from the flowers, but he also made sure they didn't take it all so the bees and other animals could have a nice taste of it.

"Do you know what the circle of life is, my dear?" She told him how she'd just learned it yesterday when talking to Aurora. "You've met the queen? She'll not steer you wrong. Lady Aurora is the best there is. But in this, I want you to see what the ants are doing to make sure the ground gets what it needs. When they cut off a leaf or a small twig from a plant, they leave just enough of it behind so it can be there for other animals, the bugs and the flies that roam around here. Everyone has a part to play, and it's what keeps the world a good place to live."

The rest of the day was spent with her going to different parts of the yard to see what other creatures were doing to help. Aurora appeared with them when she was learning about what iron does to plants and trees. The story she told was very old, she told her, but it was something that had to be dealt with when there were humans around.

"They do not understand when they fire their guns at a tree for practice, they're harming it. The weaponry they use, it cuts deeply into the fresh bark and makes a scar for a tree. With that wound, other creatures can get into the tree and harm it even more. Things like that, it can wipe out an entire tree in no time at all." Olivia said she'd do all she could in spreading the word. With her thanks, Aurora then asked her if she wanted to see a haven for the animals that was protected by the Prince family. "You must not ever come out here alone, Olivia, unless you are hiding from some threat. The animals in this place are sacred to my people and the Prince family, and I'd not wish them harm."

"I won't bother them." The gateway was just a gate at the end of the property where the woods started. As soon as she walked through the opening, Olivia felt something she'd never felt before. A calmness that not only made her feel good but also made her head clear. "Oh my, Lady Aurora. Oh, look at them."

There were not only deer and smaller creatures there, but a unicorn. An honest to goodness unicorn. As she was watching her eat some of the bark off the tree, Olivia nearly squealed when she saw she had a baby with her. The smallest unicorn she'd ever imagined.

As the two of them walked around, careful of even the small ones on the ground, she saw a dragon sleeping. A wolf lying next to him, asleep as well. Keeping her hands behind her, tightly clasped together, Olivia knew she was being given a treat like nothing else, that few if any other humans had ever seen. Sitting upon a nicely shaped stone, Olivia watched the creatures live and play together.

"They know this is a place of safety. That they can come here to rest, to unwind after a battle or a hard week.

Others know nothing of what is so very close to them, and we shall keep it that way." Olivia said she'd tell no one. "I know this as well. A fox, see him there? He wishes to give you a gift. I know not what it is, but he said he has seen you out in the yard and would like you to have something to keep you from harm."

"Is it all right with you, Lady Aurora?" She said it was so long as she was careful with whatever it was. "I will be. I will treasure it for all time."

The fox sat on his bottom and looked at her. Raising up so that he was standing, he put out his paw. Olivia did the same with her hand. When he looked at his queen, Aurora laughed and nodded. The small bite to her hand didn't harm her at all.

"He has given you the magic you will need to speak to all creatures. To tell if they are human or not. Also, to tell if they mean you harm. This will keep you safe more than any gun or other weapon can. His name is Billings, and he would like to talk to you." Nodding, she was so happy when he welcomed her to his home, for he was the watcher of the haven, and told her she could come whenever she wished. "You've been given a great gift, Olivia. A gift like none of the other Prince family has. It will not just serve you well, but the others too. Thank you so much for trusting that we'd not harm you this day."

When she was at home that night, having dinner with her mom and Kylan, Olivia kept her newfound magic to herself for a while. It was hers and only hers, and she wanted to bask in the thought of it being given to her by the watcher. Olivia hugged her mother tightly when she went to bed that night. Happiness was something she thought she'd known before but was now really experiencing it for the first time in her life.

Chapter 2

Emmie was on her way up to the third floor to see her dad when a couple got on the elevator with her. She moved back, knowing there were some unwritten rules about elevator spaces and was dismayed to hear the two people arguing. He was yelling, and she was cowering in the corner—it was loud and vicious. As soon as he punched the woman in the face, knocking her to the floor, Emmie knew this was going to end badly for her. She wanted to just get off and wait for another lift up when the man turned to her.

"Are you listening to us? That's fucking rude." She told him so was arguing in a place where people could hear you. "Are you fucking with me right now? Listen, lady, as you can see, I'm this fucking badassed mother fucker. You just shut your mouth, and you might only get knocked around a little bit. I'm not shitting you when I tell you, I'm in a pissy mood right now."

She looked down at his groin and smiled at him. "I don't fuck with men who have nothing to show for themselves except a fist they'd rather use on people smaller than them." She put her fingers up to show that he had a very little dick as far as she could see. "It takes a man with very little brains to fight with a woman half his size. Although, I'm thinking that even at half your size, you'd still be a big person. What do you weigh, six-fifty, seven hundred pounds?"

"You fucking bitch." When he drew back his fist to hit her, the doors to the elevator opened. The man standing there took one look and grabbed the man's arm before he could hit her. "She's a fucking cunt, listening in on my conversation with my girlfriend. Then she said I have a little dick. I'll show her what a little dick is." Everyone laughed. She could see the confusion on his face when it suddenly occurred to him what he'd said. "I don't have a little dick. I'm big. Like really fist sized big."

"He hit her." The man, she thought she should know him but couldn't place him, nodded once. Before she could gather her thoughts to place him, the Prince men were standing behind him. "You guys just pop in and out of places when you're needed? I might learn to like that part of having you guys around."

"I'm Jack Winhall." She knew the name but couldn't think why he'd be right there when she needed him. The former vice president? No, that couldn't be right. "It's right. I was coming to see the new children's ward that was only just opened. Are you here to see your father?"

While he was talking to her, the Prince men gathered up the woman and put her on a gurney, then took the man away. Kylan smiled at her when he entered the shaft with her and pushed the button for the floor she was getting off on.

She noticed he was dressed in a suit—a very expensive one if she didn't miss her bet. When they got off at her floor, before he could follow her to the reception desk, she turned to him. There were quite a few things she had to say to him. But instead of getting to speak, he pulled her into his arms and kissed her.

Kiss. It was so much more than that. When he finally lifted his head from hers, she could only stare at him. There was something so different about him she was unable to speak. Clearing her throat for what seemed like the hundredth time, she finally gathered her thoughts.

"I don't understand." He told her he sometimes didn't either. "No. What I mean is, I've done nothing but shove you away since I met you. Yet when I need you, I know all I have to do is reach out and there you are. I don't understand how I can feel all these emotions and not have any idea what I feel for you."

"I understand. This is going very fast for you. For me, it's been a lifetime of waiting on you to come to me so we could be together." She frowned at him. "I told you I was very old. All I've thought about since my brother Bryant found his other half was having you, my mate, come to love me as much as I was going to love you."

He turned her around. Confused again why he was doing that, it took her several seconds to realize her dad was standing there smiling at her. Racing to him, she hugged him several times as they both laughed and cried at the same time.

"You look amazing, Dad. My goodness. I don't mean to be rude here, but you must have been really fighting those drugs before. I'm so happy for you." Dad hugged her several more times as they made their way to the sitting area. "Olivia misses you too. She's at the packhouse today looking at their advanced classes. She so wanted to be here."

"I'm glad she's not, in a way. I wanted to be able to talk with you and your man here. Kylan? Are you taking care of my girls?" Kylan said he was when she'd let him. "That's my girl. She never could turn down a way to get into an argument with someone. But I do want to talk to you about a few things now that you're here. I've made me a list."

While Dad went to his room to get his list, Kylan asked her if she was all right. She nodded, then shook her head. Sure that he was going to laugh at her, she worked herself up so she'd have a good comeback.

"I'm feeling the same way if it makes you feel any better." It didn't, but she was glad he'd not picked a fight with her. "I would like to ask you a favor. When your dad tells you of his plans, please think about how hard this has been on him to tell you."

"He's not coming home, is he?" Kylan shook his head. "Why? What did this doctor tell him that I'm going to have to kill him for?"

"Nothing. Your dad has made this decision all on his own. It's something he's figured out at his group meetings. Will you listen to him?" She nodded. "Remember, this is going to be harder on him than it will be on you. All right?"

"Yes. All right. Not that I'm happy you're not telling me all of it, but I can understand. I do tend to jump in too quickly." He wisely said nothing. "I want us to talk too. I think we need to get a few things put out there."

"I agree."

When her dad returned, she was nervous. All she could think about was that he was going to be put into some sort of home and not taken care of. Or worse, doped up so badly that when she visited him, he'd not know who she was.

Just breathe, Emmie.

Nodding at Kylan, she waited on her dad. Kylan had been showing her how to use the mind thing for the last few days. He'd just pop into her head and say something to her, and she'd feel calmed by it. It was then she realized how stressed she was all the time.

"Just let me finish, baby. I know you don't want this, but I do. I need this." Nodding, she reached for Kylan's hand, something she'd been doing a great deal lately, and waited. Dad looked down at his notes, then at her. "I've been going to therapy for the last two days. I can't believe how much better it makes me feel to know I'm not the only person struggling with the things I have. Being a drunk. Having lost your mom because of it. You being raped. The only good things that came out of that were that you were back with me, and little Olivia. But let me go on here. I *need* to go to therapy, if for no other reason than I have the ability to talk to others. Not just sad stories either, honey, but life things. I talked at the last meeting, and afterwards, two people told me how much it meant to them to hear someone else going through this."

Emmie wanted to tell him that was all right, she'd make sure he got to the meetings. But she had a feeling there was more than just meetings behind his wanting to talk to her. When he glanced at his notes again, she braced herself for the other shoe to drop.

"I've done nothing since you were brought home to me. I've been nothing but a burden." She started to object to that, but he put up his hand. "I have been. I know you quit your job, one that you loved, to be home with me. I was forever calling you there. Telling you I forgot how to make Olivia something. To verify what time she was to be at preschool. You and your baby, you've saved my life. Now it's time I get out and live like a person that doesn't need to be calling on someone to rescue me every minute."

"I love you, Dad." He told her he loved her as well. Taking a deep breath and letting it out, she was going to say something she hated to say as much as her dad needed this. "As much as I want to tell you I'll take care of you, I believe you're right. I hate to admit that. While I don't want you to leave me, I can also understand how much this means to you. But please don't ever call yourself a burden to me again. Never have you been anything but the man I love with all I have. You've been ill. And I loved being there for you."

"Yes. And we both should have been pushing back instead of me depending on you too much and you putting me first all the time. We enabled each other. I needed you, but not nearly as badly as I was making out—the same with you. You loved helping me to the point where I couldn't function on my own without you. We both messed up on that one."

Nodding, she told him she understood. "Now, what is it we can do to get you back on the road to recovery? I do hope with this plan you will be able to see Olivia and me too. I don't think I could stand not being able to talk to you or hug you when I want."

"I'm going to be living in a group home. It's much nicer than it sounds, I promise you. There will be a doctor on call all the time—nursing staff around the clock. Right now, there is an opening, and once I'm in the home, it will be two weeks before I can have you come to see me. I need, as the doctor told me, to acclimate myself to no longer being dependent on your help. That will be the most difficult thing for me." She asked him where this place was. Instead of answering her, he looked at Kylan. "You know about this place?"

"My brothers Bryant and Samson have been running it for decades. While they don't actually go there to run it, they hired the best staff they could to work there, as well as made sure it's up to date in all manner of things." She asked him if they'd pulled any strings to get Dad in there. "I don't know, to be honest. When Collier mentioned it, I realized it was one of their facilities. I've been talking to Bryant about it since. He might have pulled some strings, but as your dad was going to be going there, I didn't think it would matter."

"No. I guess it doesn't. I'm just glad it's going to be safe. Is it close?" He said they'd be able to drive there in about an hour. "That's not too bad. I was going to ask how much it was going to cost, but that doesn't matter either. So long as my dad is happy and safe."

"I'm sure the hospital has worked something out with my brothers." He knew what it was going to cost but was saving it for when they were alone, she'd bet. When he stood up, she was afraid he was going to leave now. "I've got to make a phone call. It's nothing bad, but I've been working with this person for a few days now, and I have to make sure the contract is what he wanted. Thank you for writing it for us. Harper said you did a fantastic job."

"It was my pleasure. In fact, I rather enjoyed it." She looked at her dad and smiled. "I guess I'm going to be the attorney for the family. It's something I studied for, and I think it's about time I got back to work."

Kylan kissed her again before he left them there. Watching him walk through the door was difficult for her. She hadn't realized how much she'd come to depend on him to be her rock. Looking at her dad when something occurred to her, she was embarrassed that it had taken her so long.

"I'm in love with him." Dad laughed. It was hardy too, and a little rusty. "Why on earth do you find that funny?"

"Because it's as plain as the nose on your face that you love him. I think that was why this decision was so easy for me to make. You have someone there that can hold your hand. Make you happy. When I speak to Olivia about the two of you, she tells me how much she enjoys having a family. I don't think I realized until that moment that she's been hanging out with us old people, and no one her own age." Emmie asked him how he was talking to Olivia. "I can chat with her every day on the computer. She's the one that told me I needed to get up off my bottom and get my life together. I've never seen a kid so much like their mother. My goodness, girl, I do pity the man that falls in love with her. She's going to have him all tied up, I think."

"If it's all the same to you, I'd just not like to think

of her getting married." They both laughed. "Oh, Dad, it's so wonderful to hear you laughing. You seem so much less tense all the time. Coming here, getting you help, it's the best thing that could have happened to all of us, don't you think?"

"Yes. I do think that." He yawned, and she asked him if he was all right. "Some of those new drugs, they make me a little sleepy. The doctor told me not to fight it but to go take a nap. I've been doing that. And I think I'm sleeping better at night too. It's made a world of difference to me having someone care about what I'm taking and why. They explain every pill I take too, so I know not only what it's doing for me, but what the effects of it might be. I'm feeling better daily, child. Every single day."

When she left her dad a little while later, she realized she'd forgotten to ask him if he'd chat with her. Then as the elevator was coming to pick her up, Emmie realized she didn't want to take Dad's time away from Olivia. That was what they both needed. Kylan was coming down the hallway just as the elevator dinged that it was on her floor. They stepped in together, and as soon as the doors closed, he pulled her to him and kissed her.

~*~

Kylan needed Emmie. He wasn't going to rush her, but he just needed to be held. To be loved. When he pulled away, she leaned against the back of the elevator and stared at him. He felt the need to explain himself to her.

"The contract was rejected. Not for anything you did, but the man I've been dealing with for the last several weeks on this deal passed away in his sleep last night." She said she was sorry. "I am as well. However, I don't think it's as cut and dried as his son made it sound. Like, his dad had been worrying over the contract and selling to us for days now. That it was just too much for him."

"You don't believe him." Shaking his head, he waited when the door opened, and another couple joined them on the way down. Waiting until they were in the car was all right with him. However, Kylan was surprised when she spoke to him through their link. *Do you think his son might have killed him off? I mean, it does happen — more than I'd like to think about.*

I do. There was going to be a great deal of money to change hands. While I don't want to think about Mr. Carver's son killing him, I do know for a fact that he'd already taken his only child out of the will. As well as his new wife. William might well have found that out and decided he'd take over the company and get the money that way. She asked why he'd been taken out of the will. *Mr. Carver told me he'd been having an affair with his new wife.*

I don't want to sound like one of those people that are always thinking the worst of people, but do you think they plotted this from the very beginning? He only had to nod at her as they stepped off the elevator and exited the hospital, and she understood where he was going with this. Kylan liked that she could think like he did too. "What do you want to do? I'm game for just about anything today. My daughter is happy. My dad is happy, and I've fallen in love with you."

Kylan had no time to react to her declaration. She didn't give him any kind of chance. After telling him she was in love with him, she got into the car and buckled in. He stood there, staring at her until she rolled down the window.

"Well, are we going to take care of this problem or not? Also, I don't know about you, but I'm about to starve to death." He nodded and moved to his side of the car. When he got in, he stared at her. "I hope you know I'm not going to sleep with you until we're married. We have a teenager in the house, and I don't want her to get the wrong idea about us."

"What kind of idea do you think she has now?" Emmie turned to him and smiled. "I don't know all your expressions just now, but I'd say that doesn't bode well for me."

"It doesn't. But you'd better get us married soon, or I'm going to have to sacrifice myself by jumping your bones." Pulling her to him, he kissed her with every particle of love he had for her. When she put her hand on his lap, he nearly cried out. Looking at her when he leaned his forehead to hers, she spoke again. "Forget getting married. I don't know that I can wait that long. My daughter will just have to learn about the birds and bees the hard way."

"I love you." Emmie told him she loved him as well. "Do you want a big wedding? Or just something at the courthouse? I'm up for whatever you want."

"Both. We'll go get married as soon as it can be arranged, then we'll get married in a fancy wedding at our house. It is our house, right?" He nodded, loving the fact that she was getting this planned out for them. "I want my dad to give me away. I also want my little girl to be there with me when I tell the world how much I love you."

They drove home talking about the Carvers. It was either talk about that, he thought, or he was going to pull over, jerk her onto his lap, and fuck her right in the car. There was nothing else he wanted to do more than that. When she asked him if he was paying attention, something occurred to him.

"Mr. Carver told me he was going to do some sleuthing. I asked him what it was about, and he told me if anything ever happened to him, I'd be notified. He said I'd know what to do with the letter." She asked him if he thought the phone call was it. "No. That came from his son, William. I'm thinking since he said I'd know what to do with the letter, I'm going to get something in the mail. Do you think he might have written out something that would blame his death on his wife and son?"

"I don't know. Did he strike you as a man who thought one step ahead of a couple of killers?" Kylan pulled into a fast-food restaurant and asked her if she was still hungry. "I am, but this is not it."

"I know. I just needed to pull over and think for a moment. There is a big variety of restaurants around here, so you look it up while I call Harper. She'll be able to figure out for me if I'm on the wrong track or not." He pulled out his phone. "If you want to drive, I can talk while you take us someplace to eat."

"All right." He called Harper. "Also, tell her to keep an eye out on any kind of courier service that might be around. I have no idea when the letter will arrive, but if someone that had the letter was notified, they might have already made arrangements for you to get it."

"I was just going to call you." He asked Harper if she'd gotten a letter for him. "Yes. I had to sign for it. It had mine and Bryant's name on it in the event you weren't home. It's from a law firm I've never heard of."

He told her everything he and Emmie had been talking about. The will, the family, and wondering what the letter might say. When she said she'd open it for him, she did so without hesitation. As soon as she whistled, he knew it was going to be far worse than he'd thought.

"It's not worse. Why do you guys always jump to the worst case scenarios? It's an amendment to the will." Harper told him to hang on a second while she read some of it. "He talks about how you were coming to his office today, today's date as a matter of fact, and your firm was going to buy out his company. The price is stated here, but I believe it's lower than we all agreed we'd pay for it."

"What else does it say?" She told him to hold his ass. Not even sure how that was to work, he waited on her. Emmie parked them in front of a pretty little restaurant he knew wasn't a chain restaurant. He was glad for that, helping out the people that weren't as funded at bigger places. He put the phone on speaker so Emmie could hear too.

"Well, you own the company. It says that if he is killed or dies in any way before the date you're to come and have him sign the paperwork for the sale, that the building, contents, as well as anything else pertaining to the companies he owns, are to be gifted to you to do with as you please. It goes on to say that his home, cars, and any contents of the house are also yours. Holy Christ, Kylan, what did you do to this man that he is leaving you what amounts to, according to this letter, seven billion dollars?" She laughed, but he wasn't finding any of this funny.

"Has the letter been notarized?" Harper told Emmie it had been. Also, that copies had been sent to the bank, his son, as well as his wife. "It's on there that his son has been notified? Great. That's one smart man you've been working with. What does Kylan have to do to claim the business and property?"

"Wait. Wait a minute here. I'm a little overwhelmed by this. Just...can't we call someone to see if this is real?

What if his son did this or something?" Emmie asked Kylan why he'd do that. "I'm not sure. But seven billion is a lot of money."

"It is. But he trusted you to do the right thing. Obviously, he didn't trust his family." He looked at Emmie as Harper agreed with her. "Is there anything else in there that tells us who we have to contact to get this done quickly? I have a feeling that since the son or whoever has gone this far, he won't hesitate to sell off as much as he can before we can get to it."

Eating first, they made arrangements with the person that had sent the letter to him. However, instead of going to his offices, Mr. Blacksburg said he'd come to them. They were just ordering his lunch when a little man walked into the place. He knew immediately that this man was who they'd been waiting on.

"Oh my, young man, I was so happy to hear from you. I thought it might be days I'd have to be fobbing off the son and wife. She's wailing herself up big time. I'm sorry, miss, but she's not the kind of woman that marries someone like Harold. Poor man was lonely, and I told him he didn't have to marry to get what he was lonely for." Mr. Blacksburg wiped his forehead with a handkerchief. "My goodness. Well, here we are. Getting it settled up the way he wanted anyway. You read this over, and we'll get this finished up. Yes, sir, that man was about the nicest one I've had the pleasure of working for."

Emmie read it over, asking questions about a couple of places in the contract. There wasn't going to be any exchange of money because Mr. Carver wanted it that way. His family would get nothing. Kylan wondered how terrible a person would need to be for their own father to take them out of the will.

"You can sign this. Everything in it is cut and dried and at no cost to you."

Kylan put his name on the contract where he was told. After it was finished, Mr. Blacksburg enjoyed his lunch.

He wasn't sure what the family was going to do with the property now that he owned it, but for now, he was a multi-billionaire. Not that he wasn't before this, but he was more so now. It was the strangest thing he'd ever done of late, taking the property he'd worked so long to get without any cost or trouble to him.

Have you signed off on the contract yet? He told Bryant he had. *Good. His son is here. I don't know yet what he's looking for, but he's got himself a brand new car that has temp tags on it. I'd say that dear old William here is looking for a way to spend all his daddy's money even before he's put in the grave.*

"Tell your brother to call the police." After telling Emmie what was going on, she sat there a moment before telling Bryant what to do. "Have them hold him on suspicion of robbery. For now. There are a great many things we can get him on once I talk to the bank, but for now, this will work."

After getting the name of the dealership from Bryant, they gathered everything up and left. Mr. Blacksburg paid for their meal. He told him he'd been wanting to get William arrested for years now. They had made his day.

It took them thirty minutes to get back to their town. When they arrived at Bryant's home, Kylan was glad to see the entire police force was out for this. As soon as he and Emmie entered the house, he knew Bryant and Harper had been having a wonderful time playing dumb with William.

"Mr. Carver, I'm sorry about the loss of your father. He was a great man. But there are a few problems we've run into since this morning when you called me. For now, my wife here, Emmaline, has called the dealership about your car, and we're to hold you here until they can come for it." William asked them what the fuck he was talking about. "Your father had a will made out in the event he didn't make it to our meeting this morning. I just left his attorney, Mr. Blacksburg. You know him, correct?"

"Yes. He's the family attorney. What does that old coot have to do with me and my car?" Emmie asked him if he'd used his father's company money or a company credit card to buy the car. "I did. So? My father is dead, and I'm set to inherit his businesses and money. Again, what does this have to do with me?"

Emmie told him what it had to do with him, even

letting him see the copy of the second will naming Kylan as sole beneficiary to everything. William looked the paperwork over twice before he said it wasn't real.

"Oh, but it is real. Not only that, but Mr. Blacksburg has filed it for us at the courthouse on his way back to the office. He called me with the file number just as we were pulling into the drive. If you'd like, there is someone standing by for you to call to have it verified." William shook his head. To him, it was clear the young man knew he was beaten. "You've stolen from my client, Mr. Carver, and that isn't going to go well for you."

William called his dad every name in the book, even going so far as to scream out his frustrations. Even as he was being read his rights and handcuffed, he started spilling everything he knew about Kelly, his dad's wife and his lover.

"This was all her idea. She's the one that poisoned him too. You go ahead and check it out if you don't believe me. Kelly has been feeding him poison every day since they got married. It was all on her. I was being led around by my dick." The cop snickered. "Yeah, I'll admit it. My dick was what was being used, and damned well too. You see if I'm not right. She did it. Kelly did it all."

After he left and the police did as well, the car dealership showed up and was soon gone as well. Kylan sat down on the couch and looked at his brother. He asked him what he wanted to do now.

"For now, I think we hold onto the property. Since

the house and its contents were never anything we were interested in, that is all on you. I've spoken to the rest of them, and they're willing to let you handle all that." He thanked his brother. "However, we do have a couple of suggestions for you concerning the money from the house and contents. The house can be used for out of town clients that have their staff with them when they come to town to do business. It has a lot of bedrooms, from what I've seen, and a large kitchen. Or, and this one is what they're leaning toward more, we think you should donate the house to the city to be used as a halfway house for people with problems like Emmie's dad has."

"You'd do that?" Bryant told Emmie there just wasn't enough room in the place they had now. "That's why there is a waiting list. You want to do this to cut down on the wait time to get in."

"Yes. It will help a great many people, and I think it's something that would be good to name for Mr. Carver Senior. *The William Carver Help Center.*" Kylan told his brother he'd need help with it. "You're going to be marrying a great attorney, Kylan. I'm sure she can get you whatever you need to get the sucker up and running in no time."

On the drive back to their place, Emmie told him how much she loved the idea about the center. He did too. It was going to be a good way for a lot of people to have a place that could help them. Being around as long as he had, Kylan had seen a lot of people with the disease, and anything they could do to help was just fine with him. But right now, he wanted to make love to his wife.

Chapter 3

"Are you sure it's all right with the parents?" Emmie wasn't sure about this. Her daughter spending the night with the wolf pack? What if they hurt her? What if they decided to, she didn't know, run naked and howl at the moon?

"They don't do that, Emmie." She felt her face heat up when Kylan spoke behind her. "She'll be safer there than she would be in her own bed." *Besides, if she's there, you can be as loud as you want.*

Emmie wasn't sure if Kylan spoke softly in her ear or in her mind. But every part of her wanted to tell her daughter to spend the next month with the pack. Turning to the man she knew she'd love forever, she looked him in the eyes as she finished speaking to her daughter.

"Please make sure you try to make friends with your cousins. It was nice of Marie to invite the four of you over." Olivia said she thought it best that she got to know everyone living around them. That Emmie should too. "I will. Don't lecture me, child. I'm still older than you are."

She put the phone back in the cradle. Not moving, she thought about what Kylan might want her to do. What he might do to her. Suddenly, she was afraid. Wanting to change her mind, Kylan only put his hand on her elbow, and she felt calmed by the touch. Like she had every other time he'd done the same thing.

"I'm not going to do anything to you that you don't want. Even if you've changed your mind about us making love, I'm all right with that. I know you've been stressing about a lot of different things lately. I don't want us making love together to be one of them." She loved this man. She didn't know why it had taken her so long to figure that out. "Who else is staying with Olivia at the packhouse?"

"Allie's girls. I don't know why I thought this, but I would have thought Lynette might have been a little old for sleepovers." Kylan told her what was going on. "What a wonderful idea. I guess having them learning about the things you'd need to know when out in the woods is a good idea. Olivia took a few survival classes last year too. I'm ready."

Kylan picked her up and held her in his arms like she didn't weigh anything. Wrapping her arms around his neck, she kissed him on the cheek then inhaled deeply in the crook of his neck.

"Christ." She didn't know what she'd done, but she was glad for the reaction. Instead of just inhaling his scent, the need to taste it had her licking his throat and finding his pulse beating like he'd run a race. "We're never going to take this slowly if you keep that up, Emmie. I'm a man on the edge, and you're pushing me over."

"Good."

Before she could figure out what he was going to do, she felt her clothing being torn from her body. It was the sexiest sound she'd ever heard, hearing her pants being ripped apart. When Kylan sat her on the desk in the room she'd been using, she moaned when he took her breast into his mouth and bit down.

"Yes. Oh yes, Kylan, I need to come."

Wasting no time, he was laying her back on the desk and tearing at his own clothing. She knew she could dress and undress herself and that he could do the same. But this, the desperation of him ripping things, was just what her body needed right now.

"I'm so sorry about this."

He slammed his cock deep into her. The scream that she released felt as if it had been storing up for years, decades even. When he took her hard, moving not just her but the desk she was on across the room, Emmie did the only thing she could do and wrapped her body around his and held on.

When he came, she could only hope it was as

powerful as it looked on him. He threw back his head, his body bowed. Seeing his tiger there, racing over his skin like he was going to take him, Kylan did the most incredible thing. He roared.

His teeth had changed. Even his face, smooth and handsome, took on some of the features of his cat. Whiskers came and left. The greenish of his eyes darkened to almost black. The deepening of his skin, the fur she knew to be soft, made him appear to be half man, half beast. The thought of them, the two of them, taking her had her coming hard enough that it was almost as if she were being consumed by it.

Opening her eyes, she laid there for several seconds to gather her thoughts. She'd fainted. Emmie was so proud of herself that she found herself looking for Kylan. Sitting up just a little, she found him sitting in his chair, his eyes closed and his body covered in a fine sheen of sweat. But his cock, his lovely cock, was still standing high and hard as stone.

Being as quiet as she could, Emmie moved so she could sit on him. Riding his cock was the only thing she could think of right now. As soon as he touched her, helping her to settle over him, her body hyped up like it had not just come an amazing number of times.

"I think you broke me." She smiled at him as she sat down on him, his cock so thick, filling her out in parts of her that she'd not known existed before this. "I was going to suggest taking you to bed, but I like where your mind is right now. Ride me, Emmie. I want to taste you."

Emmie rode him as best she could. Each time he touched her, suckled on another part of her, she'd lose her rhythm and have to start again. Not that she minded. Oh, no. Making love this way afforded her the ability to watch his face, see his cock sliding in and out of her, wet and hard. When he nudged her neck, then licked it with his tongue, Emmie braced herself for another epic climax. She wasn't disappointed.

This time she woke in their bed. Kylan was sitting on the side of the bed with a phone to his ear. She was afraid. In that very moment, when he turned to her, she could see that whoever he was talking to had just given him bad news. He said he'd tell her now and that they'd be there as soon as they could get dressed.

"What is it?" He turned in the bed and told her everything. There wasn't any sugar-coating it either. Her daughter and the other four had been taken from the packhouse. "When? How?"

"One of the wolves, they believe. Everyone is out looking. There are even faeries looking for them. I'm so sorry." She didn't know what he had to be sorry for and smacked him on the arm. "I told you she'd be safe there, and she wasn't."

"She was safe there, Kylan. Someone from the inside did this, and they're going to regret it when I find them." Emmie tried to remain calm. To think. "She's not stupid. If anything, having Olivia with the other three is going to be a good thing. Olivia will get them home. I know it."

When they arrived at the packhouse, there were police and all kinds of shifters there. Without a thought to what he might say to her, Emmie found the pack leader and hugged him. She was sure, for whatever reason, that he was blaming himself. The man, a large wolfman, hugged her back, sobbing about how sorry he was.

"They're all right." He said he hoped so. "No, you don't understand. If we start thinking like that, then we might as well go back to our beds. They're fine. They're going to come back to us. Tell me what happened, and we'll work from there."

"I have nine dead." Emmie hurt for the families and told him if he needed anything to call her. "Thank you. I might need you later. The nine dead were killed one at a time. Ambushed while they were on patrol. Usually, we only have four or five out, but I had a dozen out because of the night class we were holding."

"Are any of the others, the ones that survived, part of this, you think?" He nodded but said no more. "All right. We'll deal with them later if you have them locked up."

"I do. At least three of them. The last one, it doesn't look as if he is going to make it." She told him again how sorry she was. "Thank you, Emmie. You're a good person." He paused for just a moment and shook his head. "Ten dead. The other pack member died just now."

~*~

Olivia didn't know who had taken them, but she knew her cousins were hurt. She was as well, but they had to be saved. They were the only friends she had right now. Not to mention, they were in a place she didn't think she'd been to before. A well, she thought, or a cave.

They were lying on stones, and the walls were also stone. Not just stones, but large rocks, rocks she was sure were as thick as she was tall. She remembered being told that no one would be able to hear them if they called out because they were surrounded by the stone. Figures, she thought. Nothing was as easy as she wished it was. Trying to get up to check on the others, she knew she'd been hit pretty hard at some point. Her head was hurting, and there was blood on her hand — at least, with the darkness around them, she thought it might be blood. Olivia told herself that since she wasn't dead or unconscious, she could still think and get away.

Putting her hand over the mouth of Lynette, she woke her up. The terror on her face had her putting her finger to her lips for her to be quiet. Nodding once, she went to wake up the other two. Hanna didn't wake as easily, and it worried her. But when she finally came around, Olivia noticed that not only was her head bleeding, but it looked to her like her arm was broken. Taking her time, Olivia asked Melissa to find her something to put on her sister's arm. While she did that, Olivia started tearing the legs off her jammies.

"We have to figure out things before we move. I don't know where we are or how long we've been here, but just staying here will get us killed." Lynette said she'd go look outside. "No. Don't leave us. Sticking together is going to be the only way we're going to get out of this. Did you see the person who took us?"

"I don't remember anything after the lights went out. I heard something but didn't think anything about it as I knew there were adults around that would protect us." Lynette whispered even quieter than they'd been talking. "Do you suppose they're all dead as well?"

She didn't get a chance to answer her.

"Olivia?" She turned to where Melissa was, and when she realized she'd found something, she and Lynette went to her. The young girl, Maria, was dead. It was her body, the body of their friend who had invited them to the pack tonight. She had been mutilated. The only thing that helped them know it was her was the clothing that had been torn up when they destroyed her body. "Someone killed her."

Taking her face in her hands so the little girl wouldn't look at her body, Olivia told Melissa it wasn't going to happen to them. When asked how she knew, she forced a smile on her face.

"Because we're together, and we're children of the Prince family." Knowing it sounded stupid, she winked at Melissa. "We have to fix up Hanna's arm, then we need to see if there is a way out of here. That's the only way we're going to be able to get back to our family. All right?"

"You be in charge." She knew what it cost Lynette to tell her that. The girl was nearly eighteen and had been lording that over them since she arrived. Not saying anything, really, but rolling her eyes a great deal. But now, she seemed to know that Olivia being in charge might give them a chance. "You tell us what we need to do, and the three of us will follow you."

They were able to find the broken bat that had been, they thought, used on Marie. Putting it against the wall where the police would be able to find it when they came back for the little girl, they bound up Hanna's arm the best they could and moved toward the little sliver of light they could see.

"That's my dad."

Melissa started forward, but Olivia snatched her back before she exposed where they were. The opening of the cave was close enough that they could run out. But what sort of dangers were there none of them knew. Olivia explained to them what the red fox had given her in the forest. She pointed to the man standing next to the tree in front of them.

"I don't know what he is, but he's not a tiger. From here, he looks like what I would think a troll might look like. Have you ever seen one?" None of them had. "Okay. He's huge for one thing and has long claws at his fingertips. We'll want to avoid him."

But they couldn't. Not really. Every time it looked as if they could get around him, he'd turn in their direction. She didn't think he could see them. Olivia had shown them how to dirty up their faces, so they didn't shine in the moonlight. At least, she hoped it was working.

Olivia asked the others to stay there, and she'd be back. Testing the wind, which there seemed to be very little of, she shoved the troll-like thing forward just before he turned toward her. Her hope was to knock him down so they could get around him when he fell over an embankment. One of his claw-like hands scraped along her arm, causing her to cry out from the pain of it. The long trip down the embankment had the thing ending up in fast-moving water. It was gone before she could worry about him getting out.

Olivia was beginning to feel every one of her bumps and cuts. Her arm was already looking festered, something she'd heard her grandda tell her once when she'd had a splinter in her finger for a long time. She didn't want to think about how dirty the claws had been on that troll. Instead, she focused on the fact that they'd gotten this far in their escape.

Melissa laughed but quietly. Olivia was glad for it. It did make it seem less serious. She was also worrying about her own head. It was thumping like a hammer had been put to it. But she kept telling herself that she was alive, and that was what mattered right now.

They moved in and out of the trees and around

large rock stacks. Twice she tried to reach for someone, but her head was hurting much too badly for her to concentrate. If her faerie was around, she couldn't find him. Everything was blurry, so he could have been right in her face, and she'd not see him. As they made their way toward what she hoped was north, the other three kept up with her. Melissa asked if she could go pee. At first, Olivia wanted to scream at her that she wanted to get home. But then, looking at the kid, she realized she needed to pee too.

"Yes. Of course."

Olivia tried her best to make this sound like they were on an outing. The girls were afraid, but they were doing what she asked them to do. Twice now, they'd had to hide from something coming around them, and both times it had looked like someone they knew, a family member or something. But she knew what they were thanks to the fox who had given her sight and understanding of things. It was always the troll things. There must have been five or more of them, the way they kept moving around them. Whoever they were, they were very tricky.

They had walked for what seemed like miles when Olivia turned to the others. Having had enough, Olivia had to sit down. Just as she was getting ready to tell the others she needed to rest, she heard something or someone behind her. Standing up, she felt something hit her in the chest. Falling back, she took down Lynette and Hanna as she fell back a long way. Hitting her head several more times, it was the blow to her arm that finally knocked her out.

Waking up, Olivia leaned over and threw up three times before she felt like she could move. Not only were the other two with her, but Melissa was there with them. Looking around, she knew that this time she was in a well, not a cave. There was no way out but up.

"You have given me a hard time." She looked at the other three and asked them if he'd put them in here. After having Melissa tell her she'd fallen and had been shot, she looked down at her belly. Hanna told her she wanted to go home.

"I do too. We'll get there." Looking up at the troll, whatever he was, she asked him what the hell he wanted of them. It threw back its head and laughed at her.

"You understand me, child? You have been blessed by the queen, I'm betting. No matter. She shall not get you back. You will be my slaves forever now." He laughed again, like a grating sound on a chalkboard. "When I get my ropes, you will hold on, and I will pull you up."

"I don't think so." Olivia knew she was bleeding and thought of something she'd read in a book. Looking at the other three, she thought this might be it for her. They were blurring in and out, and her nose was bleeding. "Don't go with him. No matter what happens."

"You're bleeding pretty badly, Olivia. You had

better not die on us. We need you." Melissa started crying, and Lynette held her. "You've gotten us this far. We know you're going to get us home."

"I'm going to try something. I haven't any idea if it works or not, but I'm getting too weak to go much longer. To be honest with you, I'm not even sure how we're going to get out of this hole with the big lug up there waiting on us." They nodded and told her she could do it. "If I don't—and I'm not saying I won't—but if I don't, tell my mom and Kylan I love them both so very much."

Rubbing her hand in her blood that seemed to be in an endless supply on her belly, she wiped it on the wall of the well where the moss was. She was crying then, so upset that she was going to die before she even got her first kiss. Looking up at the hole when something hit her in the head, she saw that the tormentor and another troll had gotten a rope and looped it for them. Like they were going to gladly go up and be his slaves. Olivia grabbed the rope and tugged with all her strength.

She looked at her blood on the wall of the well. "Aurora, if you can hear me, we're in a shitload of trouble here. I need my mom and dad. Please, come and get us." The troll above them said they were his, and Olivia leaned against the wall. Sick again, when she puked this time, her head felt as if it were coming off. There was nothing left inside of her but dark stuff that she didn't want to think about. "Please, someone come and save my cousins."

The bright light seemed to come at her in a pinhole. Looking at it, she could see a face but not make out who it was. Whatever was coming for them now, they could have her in exchange for her cousins. Trying to say that, the thing, the light, spoke to her.

"Come now. You mustn't give up. Look at what you've done just now. Pulling those two trolls down into the hole with you has broken both their necks. That is very brave of you if you ask me." She told the light she was a goner. That she didn't have anything in her. "But you'd give what is left of your young life for the others? Do you know how brave that is?"

"I don't care if it's brave or not. They're so nice. Let them go, and if I live, I will be your slave forever." The tinkling of bells made her smile. She thought of Christmas at her mom's home. How sad and lonely it was without Kylan and his family there. Closing her eyes against the brightening light, she worked up enough energy to speak again. "Tell Kylan I wish I would have gotten to call him dad. He is the best."

She was floating. There was no other way to describe it but that she was floating on air. When she was laid down, her body no longer in pain, she thought she looked around. When she saw all the colors of flowers, the way they moved around the room, Olivia thought this might be the best Heaven she'd ever seen. Flowers and waterfalls. Then she was gone.

~*~

Kylan and Emmie beat the ambulance to the hospital. Waiting for their daughter was nothing that either of them had thought they'd be doing tonight. The first ambulance that pulled in had the body of the young pack member. Marie had been eleven years old, and her body had been torn apart. The second one held Samson's daughters. Hanna was on the gurney with her arm in an air cast, while the other two were sitting in the front seat holding tightly to each other. After giving them hugs, holding onto them, they went to be taken care of while he and Emmie waited.

"She'll be here soon. The queen, she said she was badly hurt and that she'd have to take the poison out of her, but she'll be all right." Emmie had said that to him several times now. The same thing. He didn't care. Kylan was repeating it in his mind each minute too. Finally, an ambulance pulled up, and he could see the queen in the back. "Is that her?"

He didn't know but moved himself and Emmie out of the way. It was Olivia. He'd only gotten a glance at her as they moved her by them on their way to the operating room. A second—he wanted just a second to assure himself and Emmie that she was breathing. Suddenly the gurney stopped, and one of the men turned.

"Come, quickly, before the elevator gets here." They both rushed to the gurney. "We've done everything we could on the way here. She's in bad shape, but luckily she's strong."

Emmie was sobbing when they shoved Olivia and the men into the waiting elevator. They could head up there in a moment, but they had the rest of their family there, and Kylan wanted to tell them what he'd seen. Before he could move, his body aching with his pain for Olivia, his dad grabbed him up like the big man he was and held him. It was only in that moment that he realized he had been falling.

"I got you, son. I got you."

Nodding, he sort of shuffled and was dragged to the chair. Emmie was being held by Aurora, and he reached for her hand. Together they sat down on one of the chairs while the rest of his family gathered around him. It wasn't until Samson knelt in front of him that he realized he was speaking to him.

"Did you hear me, Kylan? Olivia saved their lives. My daughters are only here because of yours." He told him he was so happy for him. "I am as well. When she comes out of this, and I have to believe she will, I'm going to bow before her and be hers forever. The girls were telling me all the things she'd done for them. Even taking a bullet for Lynette. I owe her, Kylan. I owe her the lives of my children."

"Kylan, she's going to live." He looked up at Aurora and asked her if she was sure. "I am. She called for me. After not being able to find them for so long, she put her blood on the earth and called out to me to save her cousins."

"The others said she kept them together and tried not to worry them." Aurora told Emmie that was what she'd done. "The people that took them. Do you know who they were? I want them dealt with."

"They have been destroyed. I have done so myself." Kylan knew what that meant. There would be no more of the person, nor their families if they knew of this. No one would mention their names, nor would there be anyone to lay claim to their bodies. There would be none. "They were rogue trolls, six of them that were hoping to capture human children to keep them as slaves. Your daughter killed two of them, me the other four. If you knew what it took to kill a troll, you can imagine how my people are rooting for Olivia. The trolls that dared hurt what is mine, they are no more, my children."

Thanking her for her help, they were escorted upstairs. The doctor that had been called in said it would take a while, hours, he thought, to help Olivia along. Kylan wondered if Aurora had helped her too but didn't ask. He just wanted her home, safe and sound.

Every time he looked at Emmie, he hurt. He'd told her, teased her about how safe Olivia would be there. How the pack would keep her and the others from harm. But he'd been wrong, so very wrong that he wished he could take Olivia's place. To take her pain as his own. It wasn't until he was slapped in the face, hard, that he shook himself out of his pain for a few moments.

"What are you doing?" Kylan asked Emmie what

she meant. "Are you still thinking how you failed her? That you failed me somehow? Christ, get over it. Had it not been for— Have you heard a single word people have been saying? If she'd not been there, the other three would have surely died. Olivia was there for a reason, and that reason was to save as many as she could. And she did it, despite how much pain she was in, how badly she was hurt. That is what you should be focusing on, Kylan. Not that she was there when you said she'd be safe, but that she was there to keep the other girls safe." She hit him again.

"What was that for?" She kissed him then, kissed him while holding tightly to his arm. "I love you, Emmie. So very much. And if she'll let me, I'd like for Olivia to adopt me so I can be just like her."

They were in for a long wait and sat down with his family. They'd all shown up as soon as they'd heard about the girls. Samson was there for him as much as Kylan was for him. Family, Kylan thought, depended on each other for all sorts of things, but this was the most difficult.

People came in and out of the waiting room while they were there. Several of the pack came by to tell them they were praying for Olivia. He and Emmie offered their condolences to those who had lost family members. The family of Marie, her body found just where the girls said it was, had been the hardest to speak to. After so many sons, they'd finally had a daughter, only to have her taken from them. Kylan held the mother while she sobbed hard, telling him she was so happy they'd made sure her body was found, as well as the instrument that had been used on her. The bat was what told them which pack member had helped the trolls come into their home.

"I pledge myself to you, Emmie Prince. I will forever be yours to call upon. Be there when you need my pack. I am now and forever beholden to you so long as there is breath in my body." She asked Nathan what that meant. "That above all else, even my own health and wellbeing, you will be the one I go to when you call."

She slapped him, knocking him backward enough that Bryant caught him from falling. The pack growled at her, but she stood her ground. Crossing her arms over her chest, she looked at him.

"How am I to live with myself if I know when I'm in danger, you might well leave your family? How do you suppose I'll feel about calling you to my side when you could be leaving your family and pack to a fate worse than mine?" He only stared at her. "You take that back right this fucking minute. So help me— You ever leave your family to come to my aid, and I will hunt you down and tear you apart into so many pieces they'll never have enough to bury you. Do you understand me?"

"Yes." He looked at Kylan. "I think she would make a better pack leader than me, Kylan Prince. You are a lucky man."

"I am. And you'd better take it back. If not, she

will do what she said to you." He nodded and took her hand into his. "He's going to mark you for safe passage, Emmie. This is a good thing he's doing for you."

"I can live with that." She nodded when he bit into her wrist and then kissed her on the cheek. "Men. I swear to you, they're all dumber than a can of rocks. Not Kylan. He knows better, but the rest of you are stupid."

They both watched her as she walked away. Kylan loved her, and when Nathan laughed, he joined him. He told him she was a good leader and would raise him wonderful cats. As he walked away, he was still laughing. Kylan went to find his mate. He was very proud of her.

Chapter 4

It had been five long days since Olivia had been operated on, and Buck had had about enough of hospital food and the smells. Taking Sara by the hand, he led her to the elevator as he told her what he wanted. They weren't going to leave their son, but they did need to get some fresh air. They were just stepping out of the building when he heard from Bryant.

The funeral was very nice. Everyone understood why you couldn't be there. He asked if he'd told them he was thinking about them. *I did. They were grief stricken, as you'd know, but they were glad that some of us showed up. There were hundreds there for the funeral, Dad. It was one of the saddest ones I've ever been to.*

I bet it was. It's terrible when a child dies. Worse when she's murdered like she was. He told Sara what was going on. *As soon as I take me a little walk here, I'm going to send the other two out to eat. They can't be sitting around here all the time like they are. It's not good for them. That poor Emmie. Bryant, she looks like she could just lie down beside her daughter at any moment.*

I take it she's not improving. Buck told his oldest that they were saying she was doing good but didn't know why she was not at least waking a little. *I'm sure her body knows what it's doing. Didn't Aurora tell us she can feel her thoughts and that she's dealing with not just her pain but also the way she was hurt? I can't imagine, after talking to Samson's daughters, how much she did to keep them safe. And taking on a troll. Dad, I'm not sure I would have been brave enough to do that.*

I've been thinking on that too. I think I'd have just curled up in a ball and laid there for him to take me to the other side. Perhaps seeing that little girl all mauled up like she was would have done me in. I have to tell you, Bryant. I'm thinking if she doesn't wake soon, Kylan and Emmie might just wither away from grief. They're hurting something terrible. Bryant agreed with him. They were like ghosts now. *I'm going to send them out when we go back in. Even if it's to run home and get a shower. They don't stink, but they're needing a little something.*

Buck felt the touch of Kylan and braced himself for the worst. He also knew Kylan was telling them all whatever it was. Everyone would know that the little girl who had touched their hearts so deeply might well have not made it.

She just woke up and looked at her mom. She asked about

her cousins, and after being told they were home, she closed her eyes again. Olivia knew them. The doctor was worried about that with the poison and all, but she knew to ask about them. Emmie is sobbing, and I'm not doing so well myself. Dad wiped his face with his forever handkerchief and told his son he was right proud. *She'll make it. I know she will.*

Of course, she will. Everyone in the loop told Kylan they were happy for them, and Buck could feel the emotions through the link. Sara held him as she sobbed, telling their son she was so happy now. *Your momma and I are going to come back in there, Kylan. I think you and that pretty little wife of yours should go home and get some rest. If she's coming out of this soon, you'll need to be up to full strength to deal with things. Take a shower and a nap. We'll both let you know if there is any more to contact you with.*

I'll have to talk to Emmie. I'm sure you're right, but she's not going to want to leave her now. Dad said he'd talk to her too if he wanted. *I'll let you know when you come up here. Even just having her say those few words has made me feel every night of sleep I've lost being here. And I'm suddenly starved too.*

Buck and Sara got themselves together before they went back up to the room. He didn't want either of them thinking they'd not been happy with the news. However, he didn't want them to think he'd not been thinking she'd be better either. As soon as he entered the room with his Sara, Emmie asked him if he would do just what he'd suggested.

"I know I've been here too long. I'm not doing either of us any good just waiting." Buck said he'd take good care of Olivia. "I know you will. I know you both love her as much as we do. But she's my little girl. You understand that, don't you?"

"Oh honey, we do." Sara told them to get going, and they'd be right there when they returned. As she settled in the chair, she spoke again to them. "You might take a long nap, then come back here with a better outlook on things. I know that going home last night sure did me a world of good."

After they left, Buck made his way to the nurses' station. He'd been hanging out there for the last few days to get any information he could on his granddaughter. They were a great deal more informative than the doctor was. Also, since they saw her daily, they knew improvements better than he did. Coming in once a day to look in on Olivia, Buck thought, didn't give him the entire big picture.

"Her blood pressure is better than it had been. And this isn't the first time she's opened her eyes. She's not spoken to us when we go in there, but she'll look at us. I think knowing her cousins are all right is about the best news a person could have." He agreed with the nurse talking to him. "You've been so wonderful to stay here with her, Buck. I know it's hard on them too, but I was never so happy than to see her parents leaving for a little while. Even if they're only gone for an hour, it'll be better for them."

"I thought so too. Getting out in the sunshine will do them the best good. Seeing that the world is going on is sometimes all it takes to make you feel better." Amanda, Buck thought her name was, told him she loved the outdoors. "We all do as well."

Going back to the room, he was glad he'd been able to get some information for Sara. She'd been knitting while there, and he noticed that Olivia had on a pair of the slippers she'd been working on. He laughed when he saw they were a mite too big on her small feet.

"She'll grow into them. And her feet are forever cold and exposed. Remember when Kylan used to do that? He'd toss off his covers and sleep without even a single sheet over him. He'd be the only one in the house complaining it was too hot. I have to admit, Buck, there are times when I have to remind myself that Olivia isn't his by blood. She's already acting a great deal like him." He laughed again and looked at Olivia while his Sara compared Kylan to Olivia. "Also, I got her to try a little meat the other day. Just some chicken, but she said it was all right. I don't understand not wanting a little meat with your meal, but then, I don't know why she chooses not to enjoy a fine steak once in a while."

"Her momma told me she'd just decided she didn't like the way it made her feel after eating it. Sort of too full and bloated. I don't know if that will change with all this magic she's gotten from everyone, but she sure is going to need to be fattened up when we get her back home." Buck would bet that Olivia only weighed about a hundred pounds. Much too thin for a girl her height. The nurses were keeping her full of things for her body to use, but he worried it wasn't enough for her. But then, Buck had never been a doctor. He'd passed right over trying that out as a fit for himself. The boys had, all of them at one time or another, but not him. Sara had even been a nurse before. But he'd avoided the medical field altogether.

"Buck, I've been thinking on a few things. The trolls that were taking the children. Is that a practice they do? I mean, kidnapping children to keep as their slaves?" He said he didn't know and asked her why she'd bring that up. "Well, I was wondering how many children are missing because they'd been taken by them. I mean, it makes sense to me that they'd done this before."

"Holy Jehoshaphat. That never once entered my mind." She said she'd been thinking about it for a few days. "My goodness, Sara, I wonder if Aurora has thought of that too. I mean, I don't know what their plans were to do with the children once they were no longer kids, do you? I never once thought of that. We should contact Aurora now."

The beautiful queen came into the room with them when Buck called to her. While Sara explained her thinking, he watched the other woman. She was paying attention to what was being told to her, as she did everything he and his family talked about with her.

Buck knew Aurora to be older than him, by a great deal, he'd think. However, she never looked a day older than her mid-twenties. But today, he could see that she was also weighed down by what had happened. That she worried for Olivia as much as they had been. Also, he'd bet his last nickel that she felt somewhat responsible for what had happened because the trolls had come from her paradise.

"I'll get right to it. Send out an army to look into what we can find out. Thank you, Sara and Buck. I have so much on my mind of late I can hardly make heads or tails of my own life." She smiled, and the room brightened a bit with it. "I heard she woke to ask about her cousins. You must be happy with that."

"We are. I do hope you're not worrying over this any, Aurora. I mean, you should be seeing this as a good thing. I hate that this little girl here was injured like she was, but you might never have known about it had it not been Olivia they tangled with." She looked at him with a tiny diamond tear rolling down her cheek. "Don't you be taking on so. I don't know if I could take another pretty woman crying today."

"Oh, Buck. How did I ever get along before I came to you?" He wasn't sure if she was telling him he'd done a bad thing or not, so he only nodded. "I love you, dear one. All of your family have been a balm in my heart since the first time I saw you with your kittens. Never a day goes by that you haven't made me smile, given me something to laugh about and a reason to go on. Thank you ever so much."

"You just come on around the next time you're feeling low. My Sara here can make you smile when she tells you what trouble I've gotten myself into now." He laughed. "She sure does fuss at me, and I'd have it no other way."

"You old fart." He did laugh then when Sara scolded him. "There are days when I'd like to brain that old coot over there, but I don't know what I'd do without him being there with me all the time. Especially with all these new babies and children coming around."

After Aurora left them, telling them she was going to look into things about the trolls, Buck pulled out his little toy, the reader, and began playing games. It relaxed him in ways he'd never thought possible. Even playing a game as silly as solitaire was just what he needed when he was feeling himself falling into a low spot.

~*~

Olivia looked around. She knew nothing about the place she had awakened in, but it didn't bother her as much as she thought it should have. When a large beast stood up and looked in her direction, Olivia figured she was no longer in her bed in the hospital but in the kingdom of Aurora, the queen of all the faeries.

"You are doing very well, my girl. Why do you not wake up and talk to the others? They're very worried about you." She looked at the unicorn standing just a few feet away from her. "My name is Rainbow. I so love colors, don't you?"

The unicorn wasn't like any she'd seen on television when she watched cartoons. She was all white with a golden mane down her neck. Her hooves were of the bright color, but Olivia thought them to be actual gold and not just the color. The wings pressed against her sides were as snowy white as the pony was. Standing up, Olivia put out her hand to touch the nose of the magnificent creature.

"You should be warned that anytime you touch one of the creatures here, you'll get a bit of their magic. I don't mind sharing what I have with one so brave as you, but I just wanted to warn you." Olivia touched her finger to Rainbow's nose, then moved her hand up and over her nose to her ears. "You have such a gentle touch, Lady Olivia. Just as I imagined it would be. Would you like me to be your guide here?"

"Yes. Can you please tell me why it is I'm here? I mean, this is a dream, correct? A way for my mind to cope with me dying, perhaps?" Rainbow bumped her head into her and laughed when she fell back. Her butt hurt from the fall, but it taught her just what the unicorn wanted her to learn. "I guess I'm here. My body? Is it going to heal and wake soon?"

"Your body and mind are well. It is you that is taking so long to wake. You know the reason you're hiding from yourself. Once you admit to it, you'll be awake enough for the rest of them to tell you how much they love you." Olivia told the pony she wasn't hiding. "All right. You're not."

That didn't sound to her like she believed her, but Olivia let it go. They were walking through what looked like a dense forest then, and she could see the castle ahead of them. It wasn't like any other castles she'd seen. More like something from a time of large armies to protect it and men on flying horses.

"I have spoken to the queen. She asks that you stay with me until she has a moment to come and talk to you. She is the one that summoned you to this place. This is my home, along with many other animals humans no longer believe in. It is strange for me too when I visit the human world. They only see me as a horse and nothing more." Olivia asked if it was because no one believed in her any longer. "Yes. I believe that is correct. They cannot allow their minds to accept that I am a flying horse. Humans are so odd, don't you think?"

"I'm human." Rainbow told her she was no longer human. She was a great many things but no longer a human. "I don't understand. I'm just as much human as my mother is. Right?"

"Your mother is no longer human either. She is all things as well. When you were saved by the others, you took on a part of their blood and made it your own—the same with your mother. When you were given bits and pieces to save your life, your parents, Lord Kylan and your mother got it as well. To help you." Olivia didn't know who had saved her, but she was so happy to be alive. "The scar on your arm, does it bother you much?"

Olivia looked at the scar on her arm where the claw of the troll had clipped her. It was nasty looking, long and raggedy. She wondered if it would ever smooth out and look like a regular scar. Looking at Rainbow, she told her she'd not noticed it until then. Then she told her what her concerns were about it being so noticeable. Why, unlike the other scars she had, did this one stay there when the others had disappeared?

"I don't know the answer to that, my lady. I do know there isn't a creature alive, in this world or yours, that hasn't heard about you taking on two trolls and living. I am so proud to know you. Others, they will be so jealous when I tell them you spoke to me first." Olivia didn't want people to be thinking of her as something like an oddity. She said as much to Rainbow. "Oddity? I don't know the meaning of that word. But there is no one I know of thinking you're anything but a brave and wonderful person. You not only saved others, but you exposed a thing that might well have hurt others too."

"They wanted to use us as slaves."

Aurora appeared before the two of them, and Rainbow bowed down so that her nose touched the earth.

"My Lady Queen." Olivia bent as well but was lifted up by the queen herself. Rainbow left them when the two of them started walking to the castle. Not knowing what to talk about with her, Olivia asked if she was mad at her for killing some of the creatures that were hers.

"You are my creature as well, Olivia. I don't mean I think of you anywhere like I do the trolls, but you are in my heart as much as the others." She offered her a seat in a flower garden like she'd never seen before. "This is my own private place. A place I come to relax and to enjoy the morning. I have not had many such morns since you were taken by the trolls. So many died in vain when you were taken too."

"Wolves. Marie was killed by one of the trolls. I wish I could have saved her." Aurora told her in a way, she had saved Marie. That she could be buried and not left in a cave, so her family never knew what happened to her. "The trolls did it, didn't they?"

"No. Marie was killed by a wolf, one of the very pack members there to protect you that night. He and his family have been taken care of. I wish I could have been a part of it, but alas, I cannot be there for every execution." A platter was brought out by some faeries, and so was a trolley of tea and cups. The set was so beautiful it hurt her eyes to look directly at them. She picked up one of them and realized they were as delicate as they were beautiful. "I will send a set to your home for you. The magical potters in my realm, they are forever making things like this for me. Don't you think them to be as beautiful as the flowers here?"

"I do." Setting the cup back on the saucer, she thought about what she and Rainbow had spoken about. "Why am I here? I'm assuming you want to tell me I should not have killed the trolls, but they were out to kill us."

"I'm glad you killed them. They died a much better death than the ones I executed." The way she said it like it was nothing at all made Olivia shiver a little. "You did a wonderful thing, Olivia. You not only saved the lives of the other children with you, but you exposed a plot to take more children from your world. I have just come from the encampment of the trolls and found other children there. They, unlike you and your cousins, were taken when they were much younger. I'm afraid there is no hope for them other than to live out their lives here until they pass. The trolls did unspeakable things to them to make them slaves, and to put them back with their families will do more harm than good to them all. I'm sorry about that. But I can assure you that they'll never do it again. The trolls will know my wrath like no one has ever known it before. I feel ashamed I didn't know about it until now."

"Don't beat yourself up about it. It's done and over with now. That's what my mom says to me all the time about things I have no control over or that are finished. You can't change the past, so you have to make sure you remember what you did and try to make it work better for you when it comes up again. I'm sure you have."

Aurora laughed with her. "You're not as scary or uptight as I thought you'd be."

"Thank you. I think." Aurora looked at her arm, and Olivia pulled her napkin over the wounded area. "There is no point in hiding it, my child. It is there for every creature with even a little bit of magic to know you've braved something no one else has ever done. I myself have never taken on a troll without magic. You did it with nothing more than your wit and brains. People will know you for what you are. One of the bravest people they've ever known. Now, I'd like to talk to you about your magic."

"Rainbow said I had some from all the creatures I've touched today. I'm sure at some point, others, in the hospital and out in the field, gave me some of theirs too. Even you." Aurora told her she had given her a great deal. "Because of the troll cutting into me."

"That as well. It took a great deal of magic to take his poisons from your body. In turn, I was able to give you the magic that would make sure you'd be immune to such wounds again. Any poison, here or in your realm, will never bother you again." Olivia thanked her. "You are so very welcome. However, there is more than just the magic to keep you safe from poisonings. You have the magic of a great and powerful wolf, as well as other creatures that have been around even longer than the tigers that are mine. With age comes great power. They have all given theirs freely to one so brave."

"I don't know how brave I really was. I tried to tell myself that if I didn't come home with my cousins, I'd never forgiven myself. Also, I remember how Marie looked and knew that if I or any of the other three looked like that when our parents saw us, they'd die as well. I don't want my mom or Kylan to die. They're so very much in love, I think." Aurora said they were, very much. "She's happy too. I've never seen her so happy. And my grandda is getting help. That's so good for my mom and him."

"It is. He is in a good place now, and he is going to live out the rest of his life with relatively little trouble. He did not want to be an immortal. Collier told me that to know he might have to deal with being depressed for all eternity would be too much for him. I told him I understood. There is little I can do to heal his brain, or I would. For you."

"Thank you. He told me that the other day when I spoke to him. Or however long it's been. He has access to a computer there, and we talk to each other on it a great deal." She smiled when she thought of teaching him how to send her a picture of his room. But she needed answers more than she needed to think of having her grandda talking to her. "This magic. What is it going to do to me? Not that I don't appreciate what they've all given me, but I am curious as to what I have. And how I thank them too. I want them to know I'm alive and glad they were there for me."

"They will tell you the same thing I have, that you did all of us a great thing by exposing the trolls. Also, your bravery in doing so." She looked around the garden, too embarrassed by the praise to think of an answer. "You will be able to come and go from this realm whenever you wish. You need only to think of the castle, and you'll be here. I would very much like for you to visit me when you can. I enjoy having you here."

She told her she would come and visit. "I don't know how I feel about killing something. I know had I not killed the trolls, they would have surely killed us. But I killed a creature that is no longer a part of my world. I took something from this world that can never be replaced. I understand I didn't kill all of them, but they had families the same as I do. People perhaps depending on them as I do my own family. Also, I didn't get the others out unscathed. Hanna hurt her arm. I believe Lynette was harmed as well when we fell together. And Marie, she was killed through no fault of her own except to have invited us to her home. I hurt for those reasons."

"That is why you have no wish to face the people there with you in that hospital room." It wasn't a question, but Olivia told her that was it. "I see. You are making them suffer for no other reason than you're afraid. Afraid of the people that would gladly lie down and die for you. People that wish to tell you how glad they are to have you in their family. I did not know you were so selfish, Olivia Prince."

"Selfish?" She thought about it and remembered the look on her mom's face when she woke while she was in the room. "I guess I am. I don't think I care for being called that, but I can see where that's exactly what I'm being. I need to wake up, don't I? I need to.... Whatever the consequences are, I need to face them head on. I didn't think of that."

"Well, you are only seconds old compared to how old I am to you." They both laughed again. "I have another faerie for you. I don't want you to be hurt more, but Cart no longer wants to be with you. Not because of anything you've done. But he will not be able to protect you as he feels you're going to need now that others know about your bravery."

"That is sad. I liked him." She thought about asking Aurora why Cart was not with her when she was taken by the trolls but didn't want to get him into trouble. However, Aurora must have figured out what she'd been thinking about and told her. "We weren't in my realm when the trolls took us? I had no idea. That does explain how I was never able to find any landmarks to make our way back home. I didn't think they would have taken us very far from where we'd been. But to know that we were in another one altogether makes me wonder how we got there. I'm assuming magic."

"Yes. And a great deal of it. The trolls had set themselves up by using magic to keep other children from both our realms as their slaves. They would be brought from this little area to work, then put in there when they were finished with them. Luckily, you were smart enough to get yourselves out of there before you were put in the small place. I don't think I would have ever found you had you been there." Things started to fall into place about things she'd seen in the woods that night. Things, like Rainbow had said, that people didn't want to believe any longer. "You should be going home now and waking up for your parents. You've been here long enough, my dear child. If you think of other questions, you only have to ask me. You will have your answers as soon as I can get them for you."

"I do have one question. You said I had the magic of older creatures. I'm assuming creatures that are also no longer of my world. What sort of things would that be? Just one of them I can think of when I'm alone." Aurora thought about it, and Olivia laughed. "It's not that big of a deal. I'm very happy to be alive right now."

"I am as well. But one of the creatures that saved you is the king of all the waters. He was the first to be there for you."

She didn't know who that could be, not for sure. But before she could ask her, she found herself in her hospital bed staring at Kylan. He was sleeping in the chair, his body contorted in a way that she didn't think he could be comfortable. When he looked at her, Kylan smiled hugely and asked her quietly if she was all right.

"I am." He nodded and leaned in closer to her.

"May I call you Dad? You don't have to let me. I just love you that much."

"I'd be honored." He leaned back in the chair and smiled again at her. "It's nice to have you awake, daughter of mine. There are so many people asking about you it might be easier to get on the news and announce your waking up. How do you really feel?"

"I want to go home. With you and Mom." He told her he would gladly arrange that for her. "Thank you. I'm so glad my mom found you, Dad. With all my heart, I'm glad you're in our lives."

Chapter 5

Kylan was on his way back to the hospital when Bryant spoke to him. He wasn't ready to share his daughter with the outside world just yet, but Bryant wanted to know if there were any changes to her.

She's been awake for a little while. Her mom is with her now. I was kind of giving them some time alone so they could talk. I sort of know if everyone knew she was awake, they'd want to come and see her. But I think mother and daughter have a great deal to talk about. Bryant wasn't upset as he thought he'd be. *When they started talking to each other, I left them to go and get my girls some roses and candy. I think I'm getting sappy in my old age.*

Nah. It's having a mate and children that does that to you. I'm assuming Dad doesn't know either. Kylan said no one did except him now. *Good. I have a question for you. It's not that big of a deal, but we'd all like to have a welcome home dinner for her. Samson is going to do it himself if you don't let all of us have it for her. He's been on pins and needles since his girls came home. Allie finally had to have a talk with him so he'd let them out of his sight long enough to go to the bathroom. He was seriously freaking them out. As you can well imagine, I'm betting it was less of a talk to him than it was beating him about the head and shoulders.*

I can see him doing that. And Allie. Also, understand how he feels. It was damned difficult for me to leave her alone to get them flowers. I can just imagine how hard it's been for him. Even leaving the hospital was hard on me. Bryant said he never wanted to have those sorts of feelings again. *I don't think any of us do. When I spoke to Olivia, she told me she'd been to see the queen. And that she told her it was time to wake up. Also that she was magical. I don't know what she might be able to do, but I can almost taste it on her.*

Have you thought about the fact that some of us are more powerful than others? I have — a great deal. If I were a person on the outside thinking it would be a good idea to kidnap one of the kids again, I'd take a step back and look at what I'd be up against. A pride of tigers. A queen. An army of faeries. That's not even counting the fact that Allie and Samson are part of the army for the queen. Bryant laughed. *I don't think I'd want to piss any of them off, and I'm related to them all.*

Kylan laughed as well. It would be scary to anyone with half a brain. But from what he'd heard about trolls, they weren't terribly bright. Kylan asked him if he thought being a pride leader cut him any slack.

I'm going to keep telling myself it does. Do you think

she's going to be upset about a party? If she's that powerful, I don't want her zapping my ass for this. Kylan laughed again, and he realized it had been a while since he'd felt like it. His brother had had him laughing several times in the last few minutes. *You also might want to mention that Nathan wants to reward her. The pack and the parents of Marie are very grateful for her help in catching the man who did this to her. I'm almost positive Olivia won't think he needs to, but being able to find Marie's body took a great deal off his mind. They don't like leaving their dead to be exposed. Not to mention the kidnapping happening from his home.*

I'll talk to her about it. I don't know that she'll like it, but I'll try and make her understand how important it is to them. Bryant, I've something to tell you. I don't want you to repeat this to anyone but your wife. The girls weren't anywhere we could have found them. The trolls used their combined magic to make another realm where they could hide the children they took. It was a small place, I heard, that only held the children. That was where they were going to take our children. As it was, they were in the queen's realm when they were trying to get back to us. Aurora was able to shut the trolls' realm down and find the children that had been taken a while ago by the trolls. Aurora has taken care of it for everyone, but the children she found there are going to stay with her until they pass on. She said they weren't human anymore. That the trolls had mistreated them so badly that they were more monster than child. That had hurt his heart in ways he couldn't explain to his brother. But Bryant seemed to understand. *I can't even imagine what sorts of things they had done to them. Can you?*

To be honest, little brother, I don't want to imagine it. I want to just know that they'll be taken care of as long as they're alive now. Kylan said that's what he'd been telling himself too. *Kylan, do you suppose we need to train all the people in our family how to be more proactive when it comes to defending themselves? Olivia was not only able to protect herself and the other three, but she knew how to read the signs of which way she was traveling and that they had something to eat from the plants around them. As well as clean water. I don't know that I'd be able to know which berry or plant I could survive on. Do you?*

I know I couldn't. I mean, even being around as long as we have been, I'm not sure what I would have done if I'd found myself in a cave with others depending on me. By the way, Olivia was so proud of Lynette and the others. She said Lynette never once told her she was younger than her and that she didn't have to listen to her. That's the only thing that saved their lives, having someone in charge. Bryant said he was proud of all four of them. *I am as well. So in speaking on that, this party should be for all four of them. They all four got to come home. It was a combined effort that saved them. Yes, Olivia guided them through it but had the others balked, I'm sure we'd be having a different kind of gathering.*

You know what? I think you're absolutely right. We have them because they worked as a team. Kylan told Bryant that when he got back to the room, he'd talk to Emmie about the classes Olivia had taken. *Thank you. I think I'd be willing to sit in on them myself. And some self-defense classes. We are cats, but sometimes it's not good for us to shift when we need to protect those we love.*

When Dad and Mom were in yesterday, Dad asked me about carrying a gun. I told him I don't think it would have done any of them any good to have been able to shoot the trolls. From what I've seen of them, their skin is like armor. Hard to penetrate. Bryant told him he'd seen that as well. *I'm at the door. So if you don't mind, I'm going to be spending some time here with my little family. Tell the rest of them for me, but ask them to please wait until tomorrow to come to see us. We need this more than we need everyone else around right now. Understand?*

I do. I really do. And tell Olivia that I love her, would you? That kid has carved herself out a special place in my heart. He told him how she'd asked to call him dad. *Good for you, Kylan. I think you should know how much I love you as well. I don't think we say that to each other nearly enough.*

We don't. I've been telling Mom and Dad that more too. Especially Mom. We didn't have her for so very long that I'm never going to miss an opportunity to tell her that all the time now. Bryant said he might mention that to the others as well. *Go ahead. You never know how wonderful you have it until you almost lose it. I think that neither Emmie nor I could have survived if something more had happened to our daughter. It would have broken me.*

Going into the room, he handed them both a dozen

roses. They both sobbed about how good he was to them, and he got choked up a little too. When he opened the large box of candy to give himself something to do to get control over his emotions, he realized he was the luckiest man in either realm.

They talked even after Olivia fell asleep. She would do that, the nurses assured him, for a few more days. There had been a lot of changes to her body that she had to adjust to. He knew she was telling him it was magic, but she'd never come right out and say that. There were a lot of rules in larger hospitals about magic and taking care of their patients.

His parents sent dinner for Kylan and Emmie. It was wonderful to know they'd thought of them in this way. He knew he should have gotten them something to eat when he'd gone out but hadn't thought of anything but getting back to the hospital. Dad even sent along some food for the staff. They had really gone above and beyond what had been expected of them for their little girl.

"I was thinking about something Olivia told me. She said she knows she has a great deal of magic now — she can feel it all along her skin. But she said she's not going to be using it for every little thing she wants. It took me a few minutes to figure out what she meant. I'm assuming she can make herself anything she wants." Kylan said he'd bet on that. "She also mentioned her education and how she wasn't going to cheat in that either. Do you suppose someone spoke to her about that?"

"No. I don't think anyone would have thought of that. Perhaps she knows something we don't. That she could recall anything from a book at a second's notice but isn't going to cheat. I don't know that it's cheating, but it's good to know she's going to work hard for this. She'll appreciate it more. Don't you think?" Emmie said she thought so too. "Lynette and the others want to come and see her tomorrow. Allie said they have been so emotional the last few days. She thinks it's because they're afraid she'd not make it when they did."

"I think it might do Olivia some good too. The four of them are lucky to be alive." Emmie had been emotional too, but he didn't say anything to her. She would get better as Olivia did. "As I said earlier, I'm going to take the job the family offered me. I realized when I was looking over the couple of contracts they gave me that I've missed it a lot more than I thought I had. It'll be nice to only have one client and to be home with my family all the time. I've already asked for them not to pay me, but I was told in no uncertain terms that they were going to."

"I think they do that because of taxes or something." Emmie said that was what Harper had told her. "I hope you know we're a very diverse group of people, in that we're all into something or another helping people out. We've not had this money very long, but we've made some major changes around the town and other places to make sure people are taken care of."

"I have the list I was given the first day. The places you donate to, as well as fellowships the entire family is taking care of. Harper told me that if I needed to get my hands dirty on a project of my own, they'd help me get started. I don't know what that would be, but I'm going to give it a lot of serious thought." Kylan told her about the projects he was working on. "I like that. There aren't enough places like that to make sure that children are fed. I can get on board with that with you, can't I?"

"I want to help too." They both smiled at Olivia. "I'm sorry I keep falling asleep. I feel like I'm forever exhausted. But Aurora told me when I'm tired, I should nap. That way, the magic will be able to work harder than it would be if I were fighting it all the time. I'm hungry, but I don't want anything heavy."

"They said as soon as you woke up, you could have some soup. I can go and get you some if you want." Olivia told him she'd just eat something they had on the menu. "I don't know if you're aware of this or not, but whatever you want, you can make for yourself. Even if it's only soup. My dad sent us food, but he didn't send any for you. I'm thinking he thought you'd be too sore to eat just yet."

The bowl of broth with dumplings appeared on the tray in front of her. Emmie fed Olivia so she'd not wear herself out too quickly before she was able to eat. It worked out well, he thought. Both of them were looking better with every bite full.

"While you eat, I'll tell you what we know, all right?" Olivia nodded but did tell him between bites that Aurora had told her some of it. "I'm sure she told you a great deal more than we know. But that's all right with me. I'm just happy you're mending. It was quite a scare not knowing where you were."

"Dad, if it's all right with you, I don't want to talk about the kidnapping just now." He nodded at her. "I'm here. The others are here too, and we're all getting better. For now, I just want to be happy that none of us were seriously hurt. I was, but I want to think I've become a better person for it. Okay?"

"Absolutely. And I can understand too." She smiled at him, and he could see her mother in her face. The way she wrinkled her nose when she was thinking of something. When he leaned in and kissed her on the cheek, he kissed Emmie too. "I've decided I'm the luckiest man in the world with the two of you. A man could do no better than to have his little family here with him and everyone healthy."

The rest of the evening, they laughed and watched television. It was the most fun he'd had in a while, and he would cherish the memories of tonight for the rest of his life. It was Emmie that pulled out her phone and started snapping pictures of the three of them. He had her send them to his parents so they'd be a part of it too. Dad sent back a picture of him and Mom with kisses all around it, and he knew Dad had had help with that. He could barely make the television work, much less a phone.

When Olivia fell asleep this time, they knew it was nothing like before. She was smiling and didn't look like she was having any kind of dreams. Emmie sat in Kylan's lap in the big chair the hospital had provided for them and covered them up with one of the many blankets in the room. When she kissed him then snuggled into his arms, Kylan closed his eyes.

Thank you, Aurora, for my family. Appearing in the room, she blew him a kiss, and he felt it as if she'd put one there herself. *Anything you need from me, you shall have it. Because of you, we're whole again.*

I did nothing you have not done for me a million times, my black tiger. I am only repaying a debt to you and yours that I shall be paying back forever. I thank you for this opportunity to be with you in such a good way. She looked down at Olivia. *She is braver than most men. Stronger than any weightlifter. Olivia Prince is a child of my heart, Kylan. She will have a place in my life that no other will ever touch. I hope you know that.*

Thank you.

She looked at him and then back at his daughter. When she touched her, just putting a finger to her forehead, Kylan had a feeling that not only would Olivia have more magic, but she'd know exactly what she had and how to use it. Then the beautiful queen disappeared. Kylan closed his eyes. Sleep was what he needed now, and he let it take him.

~*~

Setting up her office was a good deal easier than she had hoped it would be. Emmie needed something to occupy her mind and to stretch out her body. But having help, too much help, was making things flow to the point where she felt she wasn't needed. When Pudge landed on the shelf in front of her, she tried her best to smile at him.

"You're not having fun." She shook her head and looked around to see if anyone had heard her. "They're only trying to help you, my lady. I can send them away if they are bothering you overly much."

"No. It's not that. They're getting into my mind and doing things before I can tell them. I need to be able to...I don't know. To be able to move things too. I've been idle for much too long waiting on Olivia to get better." He said he could understand that. "Don't tell them. They're trying, like you said, to make me happy. I just think I'm being overly sensitive today."

"Nay, you're just emotional because of the babe you carry." He flew away before she could ask him what he meant by that. Emmie thought about her last few weeks and how much she and Kylan had made love. Daily for sure, sometimes several times a day. But a child? Wouldn't he have known before her? When Pudge came back, she asked him to explain to her why she was pregnant. "My lady. I'm sure you have an idea of that."

He sounded so indignant she nearly laughed at

him. Instead, she told him what she meant. How did he know before anyone else? When he sat down on the shelf that suddenly had plants and other items on it that she loved, he smiled.

"You have all been under more stress than not, my lady. I would imagine now that the young miss is home, you'll find out a lot of things you've not thought of before." She asked him what. "Well, you have more magic than before. I can feel it all over you. Also, you have guards around you at all times now. Some that you may well have noticed, but not taken into account how many there were. Also, you have been tired a great deal more. That is the babe."

"Why didn't Kylan or one of the others notice? I heard that not only can they tell when the baby was conceived, but the date it will be born." He told her she'd been avoiding the others. And that Lord Kylan had been stressed as well. "I guess I have. I just needed some time alone. To get my shit together."

Emmie knew that Pudge wouldn't understand her getting her shit together. He was very literal when it came to things she said to him. But right now, she was thinking about the things he'd told her. More magic? She thought she might well have noticed that. But not in a large way. Being tired? Well, she had thought that was from catering to Olivia. That was why she was here today. Olivia had run her off when her cousins had shown up again.

"I can answer most anything you have in the way

of questions about anything. I'm very old, as you know. But I listen to others speaking, so I have some knowledge of the newer things going on in the world." She asked him about the baby. "'Tis a boy. He will be a large child, over ten pounds. And he will be a tiger, as his father is."

"That's good to know. What else do you think I need to know? Now, I mean. Do I need to be on a special diet?" Pudge told her the faeries had been making sure she was eating well. "Now that you mention it, I have been seeing little things I've not thought about to eat. Last night, I had a bigger steak than I usually have. And more sour cream and butter on my potato."

"That would be them, yes. You are also being encouraged to rest more. Until you are used to the extra person you carry, you will need to make adjustments to your schedule to rest. It will take a great deal out of you while you carry one such as this one." She nodded. Asking him about vitamins and other things she'd taken with Olivia, he told her she'd not need them with a tiger. "They wouldn't work on you anyway. Being magical, things that are human made will have less effect on you than when you carried the young miss."

As she opened boxes and began putting things on the shelves she wanted, Emmie thought of the other things Pudge was telling her. More magic. She did wonder how that would affect the child, and he assured her that he was getting all he would need to live a full and healthy life.

"Will it be a normal progression from conception to birth?" He asked her how long a human carried a child. "Ten months or thereabout."

"A tiger in the wild will only take about three to four months. But as you are carrying a tiger that is magical, you can expect to go a little longer. I would say only about five months. You are one month now, so you have four to go. Such a short time to have another tiger born to the family." He was excited, and she fed off this. "He will be born a child, as you are a woman when you give birth. But as soon as he is old enough to move around on his own, about five to six months old, he will be able to shift to a tiger. You'll notice he will be stronger than a child of his age. And that he will need to have food, a good portion of that meat, so he can grow stronger. He will also be magical. As you and his lordship are."

"Kylan and I never spoke about children. I never thought to ask. We've had something going on since we met, I think." Pudge said they had, but they were better parents for it. "I hope I can be a good parent to this one."

She was putting things away in the filing cabinet when she realized she was alone in her office. Thinking the faeries were in another part of the building she was using for office space, she didn't think anything about it. As she began breaking down boxes, she realized how eerily quiet it was too. Putting down the empty box she had in her hands, she took the box knife with her as she moved from her main office to the area where a receptionist would be.

The place was devoid of any noise as well. Not the buzz of the little wings that she'd gotten used to. Nor did she see anything moving at a dizzying speed. Twice she'd had to turn away from something they were moving, as it was too fast for her. Now with nothing going on, she was suddenly afraid.

"Hello?" No one answered her. Not that she thought they would, but she did hope so.

Moving to the front door, she was glad to see it was locked. Going to the back of the room, she could see the door there, too, was locked. The kitchen area she'd requested looked inviting yet scary, as there was nothing out of place or anything moving there either. She said hello once again.

Standing still in the doorway, she did something she'd only learned how to do that morning. Olivia and she had been playing with their magic, and she showed her how to reach out beyond where she was to see what was around her. Doing that now, she was assured of two things. She was very much alone in the building, and she was more afraid than she'd been before. Kylan asking her if she was all right scared a scream out of her.

I'm sorry, honey. I can feel your terror and wanted to see what was wrong. She told him what she'd done and how scary it was to be alone. Wholly alone. When he paused for a moment, she asked him if he was all right. *I just realized I'm alone too. The two buildings I was inspecting had a lot of faeries in here, and now there isn't anyone. Let me see what I can find out. Will you stay where you are?*

Yes. I'm not venturing out anywhere.

She didn't leave the building, but she made her way up to the second floor. So far, the only thing she was using it for was filing cabinets. But that was a thing she was going to change soon. The third floor would be for the cabinets of finished files, and her daughters and son would be able to hang out on the second. Close to her. They were all set up the way she'd wanted around the room, leaving the three windows open for natural light. Also, she noticed there were faerie gardens in each window. Looking down at one of them, she saw it had been set up with a child in mind. There was a swingset, as well as a small riding horse.

Bryant said he has people around him, as well as faeries. He's at the courthouse where he was filing paperwork. She asked him if he'd contacted any of the others. *Not yet. I just wanted to tell you about him so we'd know a little. This is really strange. I'm going to come to you. I don't know why, but I think, with no doors or locks on these buildings, we'd be safer there.*

Emmie reached for her daughter. She hated to interrupt her time with the other girls, but she needed to make sure they were safe. Olivia said they were just sitting down to lunch and that her new faerie was with her. Deciding she wanted to go home, she met up with Kylan at the door and told him where they were going right now.

"I've been talking to the others. They're all fine too. Bryant said he'd be home soon and that he'd check things out there. Also, I talked to my dad. He made fun of me for asking him if he was alone. I'm going to have to repay him for that." She smiled at him, her mind too occupied with all kinds of things that could be going wrong. "Whatever it is, remember that we're together, and together we can take on the world."

"You didn't just say that hokey line to me, did you?" He smiled at her and kissed her on the nose. "I'm going to have to get you a book on quotes. I've already given your dad one. He said he should write a book of his own. I shudder to think how that would go over. People would buy it, I have no doubt, but they'd be scratching their heads at some of the things he says."

As soon as they pulled into the driveway, she knew that all was safe there. She could see a couple of faeries playing with the planters on the front porch, as well as some around the trees that Kylan had planted a few weeks ago. As they walked up the front to go inside, the door was opened.

"Surprise!" Buck and Sara were the first to spill out of the house after yelling out a greeting. Then her daughter pulled them inside. It was a party for them. She'd never been so relieved in all her life when they told her they'd been planning this for a week now.

"I thought for sure we were in some kind of

terrible trouble." Emmie was glad to see her dad there too. He was with one of the people he was now living with. "Dad, I can't believe how good you look. Younger, and in better health."

"I feel it too." He touched the scar on her cheek and smiled at her. "I bet you barely think about this anymore, do you? You've no idea how much seeing you this happy has done for me. I love you, baby girl."

"I love you too, Dad." She put her hand over the scar. "I think about how I was hit by Herbie for those three days and don't feel the pain of it anymore. Getting Olivia out of it, I believe, made it well worth the suffering. Don't you think?"

"I do so love you."

She mingled around, with Kylan at times and by herself. Olivia was still resting off and on, but not nearly as much as she had when she'd first come home. Sara told her this was mostly her daughter's idea, but she'd helped.

"I can't thank you enough for this."

The party they'd wanted to have for Olivia hadn't panned out. After the four girls had gotten together and were asked about it, they told everyone they didn't want to be reminded of their time out there. They should have just a party. One that was in celebration of something. Emmie and Kylan had finally gone to the courthouse and gotten married, and this was the party for that.

"Olivia has been teaching me things I can use. I had

no idea about a few of them." Emmie and Sara watched as the children, all of them, filled their plates with food that was spread out for them.

"You should know that Olivia is aware of you being pregnant. When I was younger, it was called breeding. That's not what it is anymore, I suppose." Emmie asked her how she felt about it. "Me? I'm thrilled beyond words. So is Olivia, if you want that information too. I don't think Kylan has figured it out yet. I'm hoping you get to tell him before Buck does. He will too. Why don't you thank everyone and then announce it? That'll surely take the wind out of his sails." She smiled. "I'm a little perturbed at him right now. So you go on and do it, honey."

Emmie thought it a wonderful idea. She went to get Kylan and had him do that whistle thing he did so well. Everyone turned to them. Thanking everyone, she called Olivia up and whispered in her ear. It was going to be better, she thought, with the announcement coming from her.

"Everyone, thanks for helping us plan this. But I want to make a quick announcement." Kylan hugged Emmie tightly, and she thought for sure he knew. "My mom and dad are going to have a baby."

Kylan looked at her, then her belly. Then he looked at her again. "I don't understand. What does she mean? Emmie? I don't understand."

"Dad, even I know how it works. The way you

two go at each other, it's surprising to everyone here that Mom didn't announce this sooner." Everyone laughed. "You're freaking Mom out, Dad."

After that, Kylan seemed to get his act together and hugged her. Then he picked her up and swung her around the room. Olivia was so happy, it was written all over her face. Everyone else seemed to be as well. Emmie couldn't have picked a better time to do it either. Buck looked so dejected that she shared with him that she was having a boy, and that perked him right up. Oh, to have a family like this at your back or when you needed a pick-me-up. They were perfect for anything you threw at them.

Chapter 6

Kylan didn't know why he'd been summoned by the queen, but he'd do anything for her. Olivia had been asked to come with him. When he asked if he should bring Emmie, he was told the queen had already asked her to join them. Going into the realm, he was happy to see she'd beaten them there, but none of them seemed to have any idea what they were there for.

"I've been thinking about school." He asked Olivia why that was important now. "It's not, but you look ready to burst, so I thought this was as good a time as any. I want to take those college classes online like the teacher suggested for me. That way, I can get my mandatory classes out of the way before I decide on a major."

"Do you have it broken down as to what you'd like to study?" She said she was waffling between being a surgeon or an attorney. "Those are both good choices. But I have to ask, are you doing this because you want to, or because my dad suggested it for you? Anything you want to do is all right with us so long as you give it your best."

Before she could answer, the queen entered the room. She was dressed as she had been a lot lately—in jeans and a sweatshirt. It looked good on her. Also, he knew it was making her more approachable to the people and faeries that worked for her.

Sitting on the chair across from them, Aurora smiled. "This should have been done long ago, but I never found the right couple to handle this. I think that not only will the three of you be perfect for this, but you'll trounce my wildest dreams with it. I hope you'll take it on." Olivia asked her if she was going to tell them what it was. "Yes. Of course. I've been thinking about how to ask you, but I get sidetracked quickly when it comes to—" Emmie cleared her throat. "Yes, I'm ready now. I have a child."

Kylan didn't know what to say. He'd not even known she was going to have a baby. Standing up to hug her, he felt silly for not knowing what to say to someone like her about a child. Sitting down, he watched Olivia and Emmie do the same. It wasn't until Aurora laughed that he thought she'd been jesting them. Apparently, they weren't getting it because none of the three of them laughed.

"Let me explain. I have always had the ability to produce someone to take over for me. The ability was given to me by the creators. We don't have to go into why they created me, but I'm so glad they did. I've been thinking of retiring for some time now. It's been difficult, to say the least, for me to get just a few minutes of my own time. Not that I would have done things differently, but—" He only had to say her name for her to take a breath. "Yes. I'm babbling. Anyway, I have created a child like me. Olivia is about as close to what I am as anyone in the world. However, she lacks only one thing. My blood. While she does have a great deal of it, she isn't enough to take over."

The faeries brought in a bundle. When handed off to Aurora, she laid it on the cushioned footstool between them and her. Unwrapping the small blanket, Kylan saw what appeared to be a foot first. A tiny little foot. Then an arm. Before long, there was a small baby staring up at them.

"She's exactly as I am. Magical even, now that she's been given life." Olivia asked if she could hold her. "Yes, of course. I'm hoping you'll all want to hold her. She's going to need the three of you, soon the four of you, in order to be safe. I cannot have her here until she's old enough to care for herself."

"You need us to raise her for you?" Aurora told Emmie that even should they just put her in the basement, the child would rear itself. "I have no intentions of doing that, I hope you know."

"I do. I do. I was just...I'm babbling again. She

will need to be someplace where no one will know who or what she is. Leaving her in the castle with me would bring on so many wars that I'd never be able to keep her safe from day to day." Olivia handed the baby to him, and he could almost feel it looking deeply into his soul. "She can protect herself on some level, but nothing like she will need. Trust of humans will have to be taught to her. Even how not to trust others. I'm sure you're aware that Olivia has the ability to see when a person is good or not. That magic is there for the babe as well. However, she will need to learn it. I'm hoping Olivia will teach her. She will also need to be taught how to be around humans or shifters. The small things that will make her less of a standout than I am at times. You understand, don't you, Emmie?"

"You want her to be able to blend in better than you do." Aurora said that was it. That she'd never been very good at blending in. It wasn't something she'd learned at an earlier age. "I think I can speak for the rest of us when I tell you we'll do anything you need us to do with your daughter."

"I knew you would. When I was created so long ago now that I don't even remember much of it, I was as I am now. But it was thought that at some point, I'd need to retire, so to speak. And in that, someone would need to take over for me. I don't know, honestly, if I need to retire or I just need help. With this child being created now, I will have a bit more time to figure out what I will be able to do when she's ready. Where I will go, you see." Kylan asked her what happened to her when she did retire. "I will no longer be needed, Kylan. I will no longer be."

"Nope, not going to happen." Olivia took the baby from him and handed her back to the queen. "You die because we're caring for your child, I'm going to tell her what a selfish person you were in leaving us when we've only just gotten to know you. Nope and double nope. We won't raise her if you're going to leave us. Right, Mom? Dad?"

He had known that was what she was going to say before Aurora told them. Kylan didn't want to believe it, but he also knew there couldn't be two beings like her in one realm. It would cause, he'd bet, trouble the likes of nothing they'd ever seen before.

"If you don't retire, for lack of a better term, we all will die." Aurora nodded at him. "I also think you should have done this some time ago, but were waiting on someone you could trust. While I know you trust all of us, you know that Olivia, and us as her backup, are the only beings that can keep your daughter as safe as you would like her to be."

"That's right." Aurora got down on the floor with the baby cradled in her arms to talk to Olivia. "It's you I've been waiting on, child. You to not only take her as your sister but to help her be a person others will trust and love. It's important, you see, that I am no longer around in order for her to receive everything I am. You, too, will get some of myself. For your reward."

"I don't want a reward if that means you're going to leave me. I love you, Aurora." Aurora told Olivia she loved her as well. "Please, isn't there any other way you can do this? Can't you just step down and let her take over by giving her your magic a little at a time?"

"When you were in school, did you ever hear about two forces together in the same field? How together they would give off more energy than anyone could handle? Not just people, but the world as a whole wouldn't be able to live after that. We'd be bigger than that, I'm afraid. There is no letting her take my magic from me. At some point, we'd be equal, and that would cause a disaster the likes of nothing anyone has ever seen before." Aurora held Olivia and put her child into their child's arms. "I promise you I will be around for a while yet. Preparing the world for another queen. You will be preparing for her too. Her equal in so many ways that once she is in power, there will be little to no trouble from the world. I need you, Olivia. Need you more now than I have ever needed anyone."

Crying in earnest now, it broke Kylan's heart to see Olivia so upset. Not just knowing Aurora was going to leave them, but that Olivia was so broken up about it. They held each other like they were for several minutes. Kylan held onto Emmie as well.

"What's her name?" Aurora told Olivia that she'd

name her, as she couldn't. "Because you're going to be leaving us?"

"No. That's not it. I cannot name her, for her name will be that forever—a very long time. People might think I named her for this person or that. Naming her has to be done by someone I love, without influence from me at all. And you cannot name her for me. That would only confuse people when she takes over for me." Olivia looked down at the little girl. She looked bigger to him already, and he asked about that. "She *is* growing quickly. Only because she knows she is loved and will be cared for. But after she hits about what will be a year old in human years, she will then grow as any child will. It's so she's not any trouble to those that care for her. You will care for her for me, won't you?"

"I will." It was Olivia that answered first. He nodded, and so did Emmie. "I don't have to like it, but I'll help with caring for her. If you make me one promise. You don't just leave us. You have to let me know when it's time. I don't want to have to find out from someone else that you've up and died without saying goodbye. I'm not saying I won't be upset anyway, but you can't just leave us, Aurora. Please?"

"I promise you, Olivia. I will never leave you without telling you I must move on." A faerie landed on the hand of the child. "This is Hershel. He is the child's faerie. He is young as well and will learn with the child. Hershel will be with all of you so long as the child is in your care. Then, once she is ready to take over the kingdom, Hershel will become a part of you, Olivia, so you have a direct connection to every faerie that lives. Even ones born after this day."

"Why?" Kylan thought it was a good question, but again, he thought he knew the answer when Emmie asked it. "And what do you mean, he'll become a part of her?"

"Shall I show them, my lady?" Nodding once, it didn't surprise him at all when Hershel blended into the skin on Olivia's body. He was the perfect image of himself, looking, for all the world knew, like a tattoo on her wrist. Olivia tensed up, and he knew she was feeling them, the faeries that were hers to command. When Hershel stood up again, he looked at him. "You know, don't you, my lord, why she will have contact with the faeries."

"I do. It's so that Olivia may call upon them for anything she needs for the rest of her days. And when she has found her mate, she and her mate will be a part of the faerie realm as much as the new queen will be." Emmie asked why when she found her mate. "I believe he will be of our world. That he will not just be human, but he will be unaware of a great many things we all find as the truth of life."

"You will be able to call upon the army now, Olivia. Even your aunt and uncle will be yours to command should you need protection for the child. Your parents will be there as well. This is why I knew you'd be the one to help with her training because you have so many around you that you'll be as safe as anyone has ever been. And because of the marking you will receive from me this day, none of you, not you or your family, will ever be harmed by anyone, of either realm, again." She asked if she meant the trolls. "Yes, they are one such creature that would wish to take this child from you. But there are many more creatures in both our realms that will make the trolls look easy."

"Humans again." Kylan nodded at her. "I will do this. I promise you that I will care for her the best I can. I'll have two, a brother and a sister now."

"Yes. That is what everyone will think too. No one, beyond your family, can know that you and your family care for this child, Olivia. It's important you never tell anyone." She said it would be dangerous for everyone. "Yes. More so for the child."

After being given instructions on how to care for the infant, there wasn't that much involved, the four of them left the castle. They'd have access to it whenever they wanted, even if it was just to rest for a day. To come and visit. But the child would never be able to return. It would be, as many things would, dangerous for her.

The house was set up for the baby when they arrived home. There was a nursery filled with all the things she would need, as well as items for their son. They'd share a room, apparently, and Kylan thought that was a great idea. How better to help a child blend in than to have it around other babies.

Emmie asked Olivia if she had a name yet—she didn't want to keep calling it "the baby"—and she said she wanted to think on it. After telling her they'd need one for them to introduce her to the family, Olivia asked if it would be all right if she had one in the morning. They would just hold off telling everyone for one more night, and he thought that would be fine. Whatever her name was going to be, Kylan just hoped it wasn't something silly like Happy or Sunshine. It would be hard to live up to names like that, he thought.

~*~

Emmie loved the name. She also loved the fact that Olivia had thought of it. Michelle Anna had been her mother's name, and she thought it perfect for this little girl. After getting out of the shower, she went to the nursery. Smiling, she stepped over her daughter, who was on the floor by the crib, to pick up Michelle.

"Hello, beautiful." The little girl looked to be about six months old now. She was smiling, giggling, as well as playing with her feet a great deal. After changing her diaper and putting another sleeper on her, Emmie put her on the floor to see what else she could do now. "Can you crawl yet? It wouldn't surprise me if by this evening you were reading."

"I showed her how to get up on her knees last night." Olivia did that, showing Michelle what she could do. As soon as the baby did what Olivia was doing, she crawled right across the room to her. "She's scary smart, isn't she?"

"She is. But then, so are you. I have something I'd like to talk to you about. Training Michelle doesn't have to be a full-time job for either of you. I don't think you understand how much time you have to help her along." Olivia told her she didn't want to mess this up. "You won't, honey. I know that. But I think you should just work on one progress a day. Think about what I'm saying here. She's going to be a regular baby in no time. Aurora said that after she hits one year, she would grow up like a normal child. So, in fourteen years, your age now, she'll be just as you are. Aurora will still be around, and her daughter will be a teenager. Much too young, I'm thinking, to take over her duties."

"What if she's going to leave earlier?" Emmie didn't know why she thought this, but she told Olivia that with her training, she had to come into her magic as well. That would take some time. "It is sort of exhausting training her all the time. I can't imagine how you did this when you had me at this age. I have magic, and I'm still worn out all the time. My respect for you as my mom has gone way off the charts."

The hug was needed by them both, but it was the words that meant more to her. Emmie didn't think there was a child in the world more deserving of this job than her daughter. When Michelle started giggling at Olivia,

Emmie watched the two of them. They were having fun.

"She wanted her to be more in touch with people. Remember her saying that?" Olivia said she did, between bouts of giggles from them both. "Having fun and interacting with others will do that for her. Michelle will know that having fun while working is all right. I think that is what Aurora was talking about when she said she wasn't good with people. She doesn't know how to have a little fun."

"I think you're right."

Blowing on Michelle's belly, Olivia laughed as hard as she ever had before. Having another child in the house was bringing so much laughter that she decided to sit awhile and watch the two of them. Taking out her phone, she took pictures of the girls to send to Kylan. He'd gone out earlier that morning to take care of a couple of things with Bryant.

"There is some trouble at the nursing home again. About a decade ago, we put together this fundraiser to put a new roof on the place. Things seemed to be going well until last week. Or that was when my mom decided to visit there as she used to do. She noticed that the people were not out and about as they usually were." She asked him if the same doctor was in charge of this one that her dad was going to be going to. "No, thankfully. But that doesn't mean they're not doing the same thing to their residents."

They had wanted to put her dad into a nursing

home setting to be doped up all the time. She couldn't do that, and after ordering the doctor to tell them why he was doing this, they found out he was getting a kickback. Emmie didn't want to think about having those poor people comatose all the time.

After she and Olivia fed Michelle, the two girls went to the living room to watch some television. Emmie thought Olivia seemed less stressed than she'd been before. She was working on a better schedule now, and both of them seemed to be having a great deal of fun. That, Emmie thought, was what childhood should be like.

Putting together a proposal she'd been asked to do for a new playground for the grade school, Emmie wondered what sorts of things her kids would be playing with when they were old enough to go to the grade school. While Olivia was much too old for playground equipment, she knew she'd more than likely take Michelle there to have some fun. Even her little brother when he came along.

The phone was ringing when she was finishing up the paperwork. Not answering it in favor of working, she let the staff take care of it. Their new butler came into her office a short time later with a tray of small sandwiches, as well as a tall glass of what appeared to be juice. She asked him if she was about to have company.

"You are, miss. One of the teachers at the elementary school has asked to see you about the changes that are going on. She told me she will only take a few moments of your time. And as Lady Sara is also a part of the school board, she is coming as well. The children have had their lunch and are currently taking a nap. I have taken a picture for you." He handed her a photo of Olivia on the floor with Michelle laying across her back, asleep too. She nearly sobbed at how adorable they looked together. "We are not getting as much done today. The two of them have certainly gained our attention."

"Mine too. You should have seen them upstairs before we came down. I have to make myself stay in here to get even part of my plans for the day done." Sara came into the office first. She left her things in the office and went to see her girl. They hadn't told anyone about Michelle yet, so when she squealed in delight, Emmie made her way into the living room where the girls were now awake. "Sara, we have a little girl named Michelle. We were going to tell everyone tonight. I'm glad you get to know first."

"Oh, Emmie, she's just beautiful. Olivia, she could pass as your own sister. The two of you look so much alike." They did, Emmie just realized. More so than they had even yesterday. She wondered if that was by design. "I have to tell you, I'm so happy for all these little girls around. They're so much more fun to buy for than little boys. Not that I don't love them, but boys are just boring when it comes to dressing them up."

The three of them played around on the floor while

Emmie finished sending the paperwork to Harper. She was in charge of the school projects. In addition to telling her an outline of the work she'd done, Emmie told her about the visit by the teacher that was coming by. Instead of answering her by the same email, Harper called her.

"They want a new kitchen for the staff. I have it in my head that they have a better looking kitchen than the cooks do to cook for the children. Exactly what is it they want? The world?" Emmie asked her the last time she'd been there. "I don't remember. I have my faerie working on another project for me. Could you please send your Pudge over and figure out when the last time the kitchen was updated? It would help me a great deal."

"I can do that. If you'd like, I can have him set up come cameras in the room too. They're putting them everywhere nowadays, and no one should be surprised that they're in the kitchen. Pudge is very tech savvy." Harper said that would be a great idea. "All right. I'm sending him now. Are you coming over here? We can view what he figures out together when the teacher gets here."

"Good idea. I'm on my way."

Sending Pudge to the school, she made sure he understood that he'd have to stay there until the cameras were looking at what she wanted to see. As soon as he had the first one in place, she thought Harper was wrong about the update. The kitchen looked about as old as the fifties. Or even before.

Pudge put cameras in each place she wanted, even down the hallway from where the kids came in the door. It was surprising to her that no one had thought of doing this before. She would have thought that cameras would have been the first thing they put in after all the school shootings.

Pudge had nine cameras set up by the time Harper showed up, at the same time Miss Caroline arrived. While Emmie showed Harper what Pudge had set up so far, she spoke to Miss Caroline about what she wanted from this meeting. Sara joined them about the time she was talking about the kitchen for the teachers.

"I have the receipts for the kitchen overhaul that was supposed to be done a few years ago. From what I can tell here, new stoves, refrigerators, as well as new pots and pans were updated. This was only in the last eight years, from what I can see on the receipts. I wasn't here then, but my husband and boys saved every little piece of paper that things were written on regarding this." Sara handed her the paperwork she had. "But from the look of things in the school now, I'd say that someone didn't do their part of the job."

"The high school is also supposed to be all new in the way of appliances." Pudge was asked to go to the kitchen of the high school to have a camera put in there. As before, the equipment was all older than eight years. "I wasn't here then, but the rest of the staff have said they couldn't remember when things were updated. I can see here where it says they were delivered to the grade school and that the custodian was responsible for installing everything. I don't know who that might have been back then, but the team that cleans up for us now is a group called Will Clean. I can check, but I don't think they were here then either. They just don't look old enough to be out of school, much less working back then."

Emmie knew better. Her own mother-in-law looked like she could pass as her sister, so looking her age wasn't anything to go by. Looking up the Will Clean company, she discovered it had been working for the county for the last fifty years. That, however, didn't seem right either. Digging deeper, she found a lot of information that didn't ring true.

Laying out everything she had on the company for Sara, she called Buck to come over and answer the questions she couldn't. While he was on his way, not only did Bryant show up but also Kylan. It took them nearly an hour to get to the bottom of the company, then to figure out what happened to the school upgrades.

"The company Will Clean is run by Nathan's group." They didn't mention that it was a wolf pack, so she didn't either. Looking down at her notes, she explained what she could figure out about it saying it worked for the county. "They have been working for the county for the last fifty or so years, but it only started out as snow removal to the schools, public buildings, as well as the main roads through town."

"I think all they had way back then was some shovels and a few dozen men doing it. Sidewalks were cleaned up by them. I don't think that was the name then. I think it was something else, like Wolf." She told Buck what she'd found out. "That's it. Luna Cleaning."

"They were also responsible for office cleaning. They did such a good job the banks hired them as well. They're still using them, it looks like." She pulled up the signage they had used back then. "Okay, so they're branching out, and each time they do, they do a little adjusting to the name of the company. Five years ago, they started cleaning the schools. They weren't in charge when the update was done eight years ago. Do we know who was?"

Olivia joined them a few minutes later. When her daughter sat on her lap, Emmie started to ask her what she was doing, that she was much too big to be on her lap. But Olivia put her hand over hers and spoke to her about what had happened to the man and the equipment. Emmie asked her how she knew that.

Don't freak out, okay? Michelle told me. She spoke to me through a link we share. Like a baby would be able to — If it's all the same to you, I need to calm down. But I wanted you to know what she told me. Mr. Allen, the man in charge of the renovations, bought the equipment with the schools' money, then sold it off. He also kept the money that was paid to him to do both updates.*

Olivia left Michelle there with her dad and went

out of the office. Emmie couldn't help it, she laughed until she was crying. The baby, the one that had been created yesterday, had solved the mystery for them. Mr. Allen was going to be in big trouble when the police caught up with him.

Chapter 7

Roone kept his mouth shut and his hands on his steering wheel. Being pulled over was hard enough on cops. This was why, whenever he had to deal with the police, he was cooperative and polite. Besides, his sister would have his head if he even got smart with her, much less one of the fellows in blue.

"Mr. Bronson, do you know why we pulled you over?" He told the man he did not. He also explained to him that he had a license to carry and that his gun was in a holster at his back. He also had his identification there for him to look at should he need to. "Thank you for that. I can see there that—"

The other officer called for the one at his door. When he asked if he would mind waiting for just a moment, Roone said it was fine. Not moving still, he looked over at his cell phone when it rang. Telling the car to answer it—one of the best inventions of all times, he thought—his sister was talking to someone with her. Knowing better than to interrupt her, he waited for her to finish so she'd talk to him.

"Why is your name coming up over the scanner?" He told her where he was and what was going on. "They're looking for a man who robbed the store down the road from you. Are you headed to my house?"

"I am. I was." He heard her talking to someone else again. "You do know that I'm right now pulled over, don't you? I mean, at any minute, he could come back and wonder who you might be talking to when you called me, Rowan."

"I'm helping you. Shut up." He loved her, very much, but there were times when he'd just as soon strangle her. "Roone, have you been to see grandma lately?"

"Grandma? No. Not lately. What are you doing?" She said she was helping him. "By asking me about grandma. Who, I might point out, has been dead for ten years. Either help me in a way that actually helps me, or let me hang up on you."

"I'm working on it." Roone could hear her clicking on her computer. When she spoke this time, he knew she was talking to one of the cops behind him. Whatever was going on, this wasn't a simple pulling over because he had a taillight out. Or whatever was going on. "Grandma has only been dead for nine years. Not ten. I'm fixing something here for you, so you'll have to wait a few more seconds. Anyway, I was wondering if you ever visited her grave. I want to do that with you tomorrow."

"Anything you want. So long as I don't end up in jail." She said he'd be all right. "Thanks. What's going on, Rowan? I'm starting to get a bit nervous."

"The license plate number that was given to the police is yours. Off by one number, if you can believe that. I've sent them a snap of the video from the robbery to prove to them that they've pulled over the wrong man. Also, that you're my brother, and you would know better than to do something so stupid as to rob a store." He said he did know better. "Good. Okay, I have to speak to them, so hang on a second more. I'll pick you up at eight, and we can have breakfast at the diner on Maple."

Rowan and he were twins. Sharing a birthday wasn't the only thing they had in common. They were both in law enforcement. He was an FBI agent, and she was a local cop. Well, only because she'd not taken her exams to put her in charge of the unit she worked with all the time. The call he'd been on with her disconnected, and he was fine with that.

Two weeks ago, he'd been on an arrest and had been shot. He'd been on medical leave since then. Rowan had been making sure he was all right by calling him daily, sometimes several times a day, and he'd been going to her home for dinner every night so she could check him out. They were about as close as two siblings could get, he supposed.

"Mr. Bronson, I'm sorry about the mix-up. Your sister, she's a good egg. We like working with her." He thanked the man and told him she was good to have around. "I hope you're getting around better too. We all heard about you being shot."

"Yes. I'm going back to work on Monday if I can get by Rowan. She's a little protective of me."

The officer laughed and told him to have a good night. Thanking him, Roone put his license and other things away while the police were still behind him. Their lights were off, so he knew they'd be leaving soon. He wasn't in any hurry either.

Twenty minutes later, he was pulling into Rowan's driveway. Getting out, careful of the snow and ice, he made his way up to her front door when he heard something. Pausing, he felt his body tense up as he listened to his surroundings. Thinking he'd imagined it, he started to knock on her door when he heard it again.

It was faint, but he heard someone screaming. Leaning his head toward Rowan's front door, he listened with every fiber of his being. This time, he heard it louder. Pulling out his gun, he bashed in the front door. Pulling out his phone, he made a phone call he thought he'd never have to make, especially at his sister's home.

"I need backup at 24 Stillman Lane. Officer down. I repeat, officer down."

He made his way into the living room and felt for the pulse of his dad. None. Keeping his mind on finding the others he knew should be in the house, his heart hurt for the suffering his dad had obviously endured.

Moving on, he found his way to the kitchen and saw blood all over the floor and the front of the sink. Bloody handprints marred the wall. The refrigerator was open, and blood was inside it too. He also noticed in passing that the back door was broken and glass was everywhere on the floor. Moving down the hallway toward the two bedrooms and office back there, he heard the police pulling into the yard.

The first bedroom was a mess. No bodies that he could see, and it didn't appear to him that anyone was lurking behind the door. This room had no closet, so he was spared looking there for anyone. Waiting in the hall until the police entered, he identified himself as an agent and his name.

The second bedroom was his dad's room. He'd been staying with Rowan for the last several months. Mom had died some time ago, so it was working out for Rowan and their dad to be close. This room was a mess. More blood on the bed as well as walls. It looked to him like whoever it was, they had been searching for something.

"Agent, have you found Rowan yet?" He shook his head at the whispered question as the cop backed him up at the door to the office. As soon as he entered the room, the cop right at his side, he found his sister. "Christ."

He was sure she was dead. Going to her body,

he felt a faint pulse and looked where she was bleeding from. The two shots to her chest, one in her shoulder and one in her leg, made him realize she'd lost a great deal of blood.

"Dad?" He shook his head at Rowan when she opened her eyes and looked at him. "Roger Jackson. He's over there."

Telling the other cop what Rowan had said, the man's body was found under the filing cabinet just to the right of what used to be the desk she used. Telling her that he had her, Roone told her to keep quiet until the medics got there.

"Might not make it." He told her she damned well better. "Came in the back door. Fired at Dad, then me. In the living room." He asked her again to be quiet. "Listen to me. Looking for guns. I made sure he found mine. Shot him to hell and back."

Her attempt at humor was just like his sister. When the chips were down, he knew she'd make a joke. She told him in broken sentences what had happened. Jackson wanted guns and figured a cop would have plenty. If he'd gotten to the basement, he would have found her safe, but getting into it would have been impossible.

The medics started to work on her as soon as they got there. Roone didn't leave the room even when ordered to. She was his sister, and there wasn't any way he was going to leave her now. The police worked in the other parts of the house while he waited on them to tell him she was going to make it. Or if she wasn't. No one, it seemed, wanted to make that call.

"Agent Bronson, do you have any idea why someone would target your family?" Roone told the cop what Rowan had told him. "Does she have guns on the premises?"

He told the man he didn't live there. He knew she had guns, a great deal of them. They had been their dad's and his dad's before him. They were a family of cops. He was the only one that had gone a slightly different direction and became a Fed. But he would never volunteer that sort of information to anyone. Not if he could help it.

As they rolled her out of the room, he followed. When one of the officers that pulled him over earlier stopped him, a thought occurred to him. He would have been there, too, had they not pulled him over. He didn't know if that meant he would have been killed too or could have helped his family, but he asked the man what he needed.

"I'm sorry." Roone told him he had to go. "You might have saved her. You could have been here when someone broke in."

"I might well have been killed as well. She'll be fine. I can't help but think that. All right?"

He was out the door before anyone else could talk to him. His dad was gone too, he remembered at the last second, and wondered what the hell he was going to do if something happened to his sister.

Driving to the hospital, he made some phone calls. First, he called Margie, their older sister. She said she'd meet him at the hospital. Then he called Micky, his younger sister. Micky was younger than he was by only eleven months. She said she'd get a ride with Margie and would see him there. None of them asked about Dad, and he didn't tell them yet. Just them worrying about Rowan was hard enough. Calling his brother, he had to wait for several minutes before he was able to come to the phone. Mark worked at the hospital he was headed to.

"She's on her way up to surgery. It's bad—you know that, don't you?" He said he was the one that had found her. "I guess you've heard that Dad didn't make it. Christ, this is a nightmare. What the fuck would they want shooting up an old man and our sister?"

"Guns." Mark told him he had to go, that the ER was busy, and Roone said he'd be there in five minutes. Just as he was walking in the door, he saw his sisters pulling in too. Pulling out his cell phone, he called the other two siblings. They were a large family, he thought with a small grin. Calling Jeff and Winnie, he figured by the time they arrived, everyone in the county would know that Rowan had been shot. He hated to tell them about Dad, but it had been left up to him to spread the news. Roone also called Rowan's boss and friend of the family.

"I just heard. I'm so sorry for your loss, Roone. You need anything to help that girl along, you tell me."

He said he would. "She's just too stubborn to die, you know that, don't you? That red hair of hers, it's not just for show. Rowan has a temper like nobody has ever seen before, I tell you that."

"I've called the rest of them in. We're all redheads, you know." He said he knew that too and thought their parents must have been saints to have so many high tempered people in one household. "Mostly, it was Micky and Rowan that were high tempered. I have to go, my sisters are needing me, sir. I'll keep you updated. Mark said they took her right up to surgery, and we might not hear anything for a while."

"You do that, son. You keep me informed."

Roone made sure he had his cell phone number. Hanging up after getting told everyone was praying for his sister, Roone prepared himself for a long wait. She couldn't die. Not her. She was his other half. His twin in all things.

There was no word coming from the operating room. Mark called him twice, once to tell him he was working over and would be up soon. Then the second time, to let him know that Dad's body had arrived and they were going to perform an autopsy on it as soon as possible. He had told the others Dad had been murdered but kept the fact that Dad had suffered badly to himself.

The surgery took seven hours to finish up. The surgeon, via his nurse, told them she'd be down to see them as soon as she got Rowan set up in ICU. The nurse that had spoken to them said she'd not been in the operating room, so had no information to give them. It was just as well, he thought. She'd not be able to answer any of the harder questions he knew Mark would ask. He was a stickler for details.

They were taken to a large room that had a single table, as well as a couple of vending machines. Once they were all seated, he got up and put the pocket full of change he'd taken from his car into the machine and got all of them drinks. It had been a long night so far, and he, for one, could use a little pick up in the way of some caffeine. The doctor, Doctor Margery Fleming, came in just as he was getting himself another drink.

"I'm not one to pull punches here, so if that's the way you want it, in bits and pieces, you might as well leave the room now." No one moved. "Good. All right. Rowan was shot a total of eight times. I've taken out six of the bullets, but the others didn't stick around. Through and through is all I can figure. She was shot twice in the chest, once in both knees, as well as in her left elbow. There were two to her head, as well as one that hit her in her left hand. He was bound and determined, it looks like to me, that she suffered. She has lost a great deal of blood, so if you all wouldn't mind giving a little back to us, that'll be great."

Doctor Fleming pulled out photos and handed them around to them. "While I don't normally take pictures of my patients, I was asked to do so by the officer in charge of the investigation. As you can see from the photos there, the bullet to her head was what worried me the most. However, after starting there, we ascertained that no brain damage was evident so far. The bullet only cracked her skull but didn't penetrate her brain." He asked about the chest wounds. "Did you notice that she had on her vest when you found her, Agent? It wasn't done up, buckled in place, so I'm assuming when she heard the shots that took your father, she pulled it on. Smart chicky there."

He'd not noticed but remembered seeing it now that it was mentioned. Letting out a long breath, he felt like she might just make it after all. The doctor was talking about the next forty-eight hours and what it would mean for her. Mark had more questions, but the one they all heard him ask was what they wanted to hear.

"Will she make it? I honestly have no idea. She's young, strong, and in great shape. However, as I said, she's been shot to fuck and lost a great deal of blood." Roone asked the doctor what her odds were. "Sixty/ forty that she won't make it. I'm very sorry. I wish I had better odds, but as I said, the next two days will tell us a great deal."

"She'll make it. Simply because the odds are against her that she won't." He grinned at Micky when she spoke up. "My dad, he was brought in. Do you have any information on how he was murdered?"

"No. I know the coroner and that he's damned

good at his job. However, I was told this was a drug-related crime. That someone was looking for guns to sell. I don't buy that. I've seen a lot of people suffer for a great deal more than just a few guns. There is more to this than what the police are saying." She looked at him. "You're a cop too, I've heard. I'd keep an open mind if I were you, Roone. Something just ain't right in the pudding I've been served."

"Thank you for that."

She left them there, telling them she was going to check on Rowan again. After she was gone, Roone called Jeff to let him know what they knew. He said he and Winnie would be landing in twenty minutes, then they'd come straight there.

Roone hated to take them away from their work, but he was thrilled that they dropped everything to be there. They were close, he thought. Angry most of the time at one or more of each other, but they came together when it was needed. Roone knew they would need each other in the coming hours more than ever before.

~*~

Kylan helped Marcus take the furniture out of the barn. It had been stored there while he had his home repainted. The two of them had been working for the last few hours and not saying a word. Marcus finally turned and looked at him with a smile. The office the two of them worked in, the advertising company, was just about ready to open. They'd taken their time in setting things up so it would be a good place to work.

"You've never been one to empty your head when we're together. If any of the others were helping me, especially Bryant, I'd be sending him home by now. Christ, he can sure talk your arm off." Kylan told his brother that Dad would have been worse. "Yes. He would have wanted to know where I was putting this stuff in the house. I have it all set up in my mind right now, but nothing is etched in stone yet."

Marcus had bought Bryant's former boss's home, fully furnished, when it went on the market. It wasn't at all what he thought it was going to be like, but wood and slate. Colors of nature as well. Having all the furniture removed had been Mom's idea so it could be cleaned. The stuff looked brand new to him.

Putting things away once they were able to get them in the rooms, he didn't envy his brother all the work that needed to be done yet. The staff, he knew, would be his biggest help. However, there was still a great deal of clothing, personal things, as well as the wine cellar in the lower levels. All in all, it was going to be a chore for all of them.

"Your daughters are beautiful. I meant to tell you that the other day, but I kept getting sidetracked with the move into the offices." He said he loved them very much already. "I can see that. Michelle is about the most adorable baby I've ever seen. And she loves Olivia. They're inseparable, aren't they?"

"Yes. They started watching television together in Olivia's room one night, and now she sleeps in there with her. I think Emmie is slightly jealous of their relationship. I know I am a little. But that is why we have her. So that she'll be happy and well liked." Everyone knew what was going on with the little girl. Of course, he'd not had to tell them that no one else was to know. They seemed to get that on their own. What did surprise him, however, was how much Michelle was looking like she had been born to them. Even her hair color was now a dark black like his. "It's fun having two little girls in the house. Sort of like having a party all the time."

"Do you suppose your son will be hanging out with them?" He said he thought he might at first, but as they all got older, they'd go their separate ways. "I can see that happening. Remember how much we hung out with the Sanders girls? They were fun until they started figuring out that boys were kinda neat."

Leave it to Marcus to say something like that. They spoke about the new businesses going in around town, as well as the office Emmie was setting up. She had converted the entire upstairs into a living room/kitchen so the kids could come over and be close by. He had already noticed that Olivia had made some of the space her own little domain.

They were getting ready to part ways when Bryant came to see him. Kylan was almost afraid of what he had to tell him. So when he asked if he had any plans for the day, he nearly told him he did. Whatever was going on, Bryant was extremely upset about it. In a stressful way, not angry.

"A friend of mine called me just a little while ago. She's a surgeon at a hospital in the Cleveland area. Margery has this woman in her hospital that isn't going to make it without a little help from us. She's a good cop, as well as a sister to some really wonderful people. She doesn't want her to die." Kylan told him he'd do whatever was needed. "I was hoping you'd say that. She's been shot to fuck—not my words, but Margery's. She's not one to butter you up before she shoots you with the truth. The family lost their father in the shooting, and it would devastate the community as well as this family if they were to lose her too. She's a decorated officer, as well as someone I'd like to see in action."

"I'm assuming we're leaving right now." He nodded, and Kylan followed him out to his car. "I really didn't have anything planned. Just to spend the night at home. But I would have cancelled them to help you out with this."

"I thank you for that. I've already cleared helping her with Aurora. I mean, she's not a cat or one of us, so I didn't know if I could go and help her. She said for us to hurry."

Nodding, he reached out to Emmie to let her know what was going on.

Yes, you need to be there. Do whatever you need. He

said he didn't know how long he'd be. *That's no trouble here. The girls and I will make an evening or two of it, and when you return, we'll have a nice family dinner together. With everyone.*

That would be wonderful. Marcus might need a little help at his home. We were just getting started on putting away some of the linens and things he'd purchased for his new place. She said she'd go over and help him out when she was finished there. *We need to get you a car too. I've been thinking I might want to invest in one myself. It's going to be tough getting three kids in the truck with two in car seats. What do you think?*

I'll do some research on them while you're gone. Be careful, and tell Bryant I think what he is doing is great. After closing the connection, he told his brother what was going on. They were getting on the highway when Emmie reached out to him again. *This woman, is her name Rowan Bronson by any chance?*

He asked Bryant, and he said he didn't think to ask. *We don't know. Why? Did you find something while you were online? You're supposed to be working, you know.* He laughed but was worried when Emmie didn't join him.

I was working, but this news flash thing came up on my computer. She was shot in her home, the paper says. That not only could she lose her life, but her father was killed as well. She shot the intruder, but not before he shot her several times. She's one of seven children. And a twin of Roone Bronson. I know of him. He's a big deal in the Feds world. He told Bryant what he was learning from Emmie. *If this is her, you'd better do whatever it takes to make sure she lives, Kylan. This is one of the good ones. Not just her, but the entire family. In addition to Roone being a Fed, they range from an operator for an elderly daycare center, two doctors, as well as two of them work at building homes in other countries.*

Christ. He told Bryant why this was so important. "What do you want to do? I mean, we can't change her, but we can give her enough of our blood to make sure she lives. I know I can heal her wounds. By accident, I figured out that with just dropping a bit of my blood onto a bad wound, it will heal immediately."

"Heal her. Save her. That's all I want to do with this." Bryant drove for a little while longer before speaking again. "Do you suppose any one of them could be Harley or Marcus's mate? Not that it matters, but it seems they're on board with all the things we take care of. It would be a good fit."

"I wouldn't mention that to them or to our brothers. That might mean an all-out family gathering up there." They were both laughing when they saw the signs for Cleveland. "Another hour, I guess. That's not too bad. Let's just not end up in the ER with her by hurrying too much. Besides, since you're driving, Emmie will take you apart if I get hurt."

"You wussy." Marcus had been right about Bryant talking all the time. But most of it was speculations on the new things they were getting into. The halfway house was just one of many topics they went over. Kylan was excited, now that the building he was going to be working from was brought up to this century, that he'd be able to get started on a lot of things. "Mom is making sure that the not for profit programs are up and running. I'd forgotten how good she was at getting people to donate. We should have enough coats and mittens to give to every person in town, with some leftover for next year, at the rate she's going. She's already starting on next year's food drive. A lot of people can use that this year too."

By the time they were pulling into the hospital parking lot, Kylan had notes on things he was going to make up an ad campaign for. Also, they were going to hire more staff for the cable company. A project within a project there.

They were trying a new scheduling program, with people working half shifts and some people on call. It was working out very well too. So instead of one cable office carrying the entire load for them, all the offices were doing very well. Bryant had also started running classes on how to fix remotes. Also, how to tell when someone was just lonely and needed someone to talk to.

Doctor Fleming met them at the door. "The family would like a quick word with you about their sister. I told them you were going to have to do some of your magic on her, and they're all right with it. However, they still want to meet the two of you." Bryant told her that was fine. "I didn't think you'd mind. Thank you so much for this. You've no idea how special this young lady is to so many people."

The room they were led to was filled to overflowing. Kylan could tell the siblings because they all had the reddest hair he'd ever seen. It wasn't orange like he'd thought of with a person being a redhead, but a lovely shade of dark red. He shook hands with each of them, getting just a little information about each.

"We've spoken, the six of us, and we're all for whatever you can do to give our sister back to us." Mark, the oldest, and by far the most nervous, introduced them to his family. "We have to bury our father soon, and this would be.... If we lose her too, I just don't know how we'll cope. I'm sure you can understand where we're coming from."

"Yes. We have families too. As both of us are powerful beings, you have to understand that when we heal her, we'll be using magic. The kind that few people have ever seen. We're not sure what it will do to her. What she'll be able to do because of it." Roone said so long as she was with them, they didn't care if she could jump off buildings and fly. "I don't know if she'll be able to do that, but like I said, we just don't know."

He didn't tell them she'd not be able to fly. Kylan wasn't going to make any kind of promises. When they entered the room where she was, Kylan had to stand back for a moment just to take in the number of machines hooked up to her and the damage done to her body. He understood now why he and Bryant had been asked to come here. The two of them got to work immediately.

Chapter 8

Micky sat in the little room that had been opened up for them. She was sick with worry about her sister and didn't want her to die. She supposed they all wanted that, but she and Rowan were close. They told each other everything.

"Oh, I'm sorry. I didn't know anyone was in here." She told Kylan to come and join her. That she could use some company. "All right. If you don't want me here, just say so. I'm sure I can find someplace else." His smile was reassuring.

"Rowan and Roone are only eleven months older than me. The others are about two years apart from the next one. Jeff and Winnie are twins as well." He told her that must have been wonderful growing up. "It was. We were never alone. None of us have ever been without someone we can depend on. Rowan is my go-to gal when I need a shoulder or just to let off steam. She was good at that. Helping you let off some steam to her."

"You were told what we did for her, weren't you?" She nodded and looked down at her water bottle. "I made sure her knees were repaired. I may have to go back in again and make sure her bones are healing the way they should. Bryant, he made sure the rib that pierced her lung was moved and put in place before healing her lungs. I guess I never thought of how much damage could happen to a person even with a vest on."

"As close as we were told he was to her, it's small wonder he didn't break more than that. Three ribs aren't that many when you get shot twice in the chest at close range." Kylan nodded and said he'd have more respect for cops now because of it. "My father was a cop. His father too, and so far back, I have a feeling we might well have been the very first ones. Not really, but it's a family thing. Dad didn't care if any of us carried on the tradition so long as what we did made us want to do it every day. And if it didn't, then find something that did. That's one of the reasons I'm selling my daycare to someone right now. I've found that now I've taken it about as far as I can go with it, I want to move on."

"What do you think you'll do now? If you don't mind me asking." She said she was still working on that but didn't mind him asking at all. "We all tried a little of everything while we grew up. I couldn't draw a stick person well when I started out drawing, but I've had a lot of time to work on it. Now I think I'm pretty good. I had to really work at it. However, it's something I still enjoy. Advertising is a fun way to make a living."

"Bryant mentioned that you were all very old. And the first black tigers. I've never seen one in real life. Just pictures. They're so different than Bengals, aren't they?" He told her they were even larger than the ones in zoos too. "I can't imagine how you were able to go from being a little kitten to what you are today. It must have— My mind is blown by what sorts of things you've seen change since you were born. What was the biggest change that wowed you?"

"Everything, really. The first time we saw electricity was terrifying for us. Then there were cars that moved down the road. Antibiotics were the biggest, best thing I can think of. So many people died from a simple cut that wouldn't even need any kind of assistance from a doctor nowadays. Trains too. I used to love riding on them. Not the kind now that will pamper to your every need, but just hitching a ride on one of the carts to get from one point to the next. I didn't even have to have a place to go. I just enjoyed the ride." Micky laughed and was glad that he'd come to sit with her. "There aren't as many changes as there used to be. Still, they happen, but not on the level they did then. What do you enjoy doing?"

"I'm the black sheep of the family, you might say. I am forever looking for the next project I can immerse myself in. I've started and moved on to more projects than all of the others together. It's what I do." He asked her if she enjoyed that. "I used to. Not so much anymore. I have money, a great deal of it. We all do. It's not like I start these projects, then just walk away. I get them up and running, then hire someone else to take over. I have my toes in a lot of water all the time."

"Good for you." They both laughed, and when Bryant joined them, he asked his brother if he was ready to go back to Rowan. "Would you like to come with us? I know you've all declined to see her like she is, but she looks a good deal better than when we came in. We were warned not to heal her completely, for the press, but unless something else happens to her at this point, she'll live."

"I think I would." When she stood up, she followed them out of the room. "Rowan is my best sister. I need her like I need air to breathe."

"I know just how you feel." The room was dark when they entered. It wasn't until they told her why that she understood. "Having the lights off in here doesn't bring us any unwanted attention while we're with her. Some people might have seen us going back and forth, but we've made it so they don't know our faces when we leave here."

"I would imagine this sort of thing could get you a lot of kooks coming around wanting you to heal every Tom, Dick, and Harriet they know." Micky moved up to the bed to look at her sister. "She does look better. When Doctor Fleming showed us pictures of her, I decided

I didn't want to see her in person. That guy, he did a number on her."

"Yes, she was lucky her vest was nearby." Touching her fingers to her sister's cheek, she half listened to the other two as they gave Rowan more of their magic. They were telling her sister what they were doing, how it was going to affect her, as well as some of their personal information. Kylan had two little girls and a son on the way. She was—

"Guys?" Neither of them said anything when she called for them. "Guys, she's staring at me. My sister is looking at me right now."

"Talk to her." Nodding, nothing at all came to mind. If asked, Micky wasn't even sure she could have told Rowan what the weather was like, much less the date. "Go ahead, Micky. Tell her how much you miss her."

"I do." She leaned closer as Rowan looked at her. "You're going to get better, and we're going to go on the cruise we promised we'd go on. Remember?"

She blinked twice at her, and Micky laughed and cried. Leaning down to kiss her on her forehead, Micky whispered how much she loved her. Rowan's hand moved, and reaching for it, Micky held onto it for several seconds while they looked at each other. The tube in her mouth, helping her breathe from the lung injury, prevented Rowan from speaking, but the two of them were able to convey volumes in just those short few minutes. Then Rowan closed her eyes and drifted into what she hoped was a better sleep than before.

"You were lucky today." She nodded, unable to speak to Kylan when he spoke to her. "In my family, they'd be so jealous that you'd been able to talk to her. She'll get better more and more now that she's on her way. I'm betting soon they'll take the tubing out, and she'll be able to breathe on her own."

Micky knew they were each giving Rowan blood. Not very much, just a few drops she'd been told. But it was working wonders on her. Working to bring her sister to them again. Not wanting to leave her, but knowing she had to when they did, she stood outside the room and sobbed.

It was going to be all right, she told herself. Rowan would be her old self in no time, and they really would go on that trip. Making her way back to the little room she'd been in, she was both dismayed and happy that Roone was there. Telling him what had happened, the two of them held each other as they cried.

"The first thing I'm going to make her do is to get better locks on her doors. Not to mention stronger doors." Micky told Roone she'd more than likely not want to live in the house any longer. "I never thought of that. You're more than likely right. I don't know that I'd want to live there either. Although, perhaps she'll want to live with one of us for a little while. Just until she's up and around for a while."

"She won't want to do that either, Roone. If she's up and around even a little, you know her well enough to understand she'd want to live on her own. That way, no one can tell her when she should rest." Roone laughed with her. "I'm betting in no time at all she'll be taking on cases from wherever she's living and solving them too. There is no stopping a Bronson when they can use a phone."

They sat there for a little while longer, just the two of them. Kylan came in once and said they would see to Rowan once more before they left. The two of them had refused any kind of payment from them, not even for their hotel. She thought if the rest of the family were anything like these two, she might like to meet them. When Jeff and Winnie showed up, they were told about Rowan, too, while Micky drifted down to the cafeteria area of the hospital. She just needed a moment of quiet time before she went home. The six of them were taking turns staying with Rowan so they could get some rest and food. Her turn wouldn't be again until tomorrow morning. But she needed this time just to sit and think.

There was too much going on right now for her to rest well. Not only did she want to be there for Rowan, but the others too. What she'd not told Kylan was that she'd put her daycare center on the market and was in the process of selling it now. Just walking away from a business was something she rarely did. Usually, she would hire someone to take it over while she reaped the profits. She didn't want to do that this time.

Going home, Micky pulled her laptop to her while she was resting on the couch. She looked up the Prince family and was impressed with the things they were into. The picture of them all together at what looked like a wedding showed six big men and a mom and dad. She wondered, like everyone did, she was sure, how they had gone for so long not finding their wives, being as old as they were.

She supposed that waiting on one's other half—their mates, as they were called—took time. Micky didn't think she'd ever marry again. The first one, lasting only five weeks, had ended abruptly when he was killed by a drive-by shooting. She'd not even dated all that much since then and wondered why.

"Oh yeah. Men are pigs." She smiled at her reasoning and thought of all the shit she was going to have to do now that she didn't have anywhere to go. It wasn't like she'd not be able to find herself a job, but she didn't want to right now. "Maybe I'll take a few days and just drive around the state."

Her cat, a small house cat, came and sat near her on the couch. He wouldn't get up with her no matter how many times she told him it was all right. After figuring out what was going on, she laughed until she was crying. The cat knew she'd been around a bigger cat, and he was jealous.

"You might as well join me here, Becket. He's not

going to come around once Rowan is well." Still, he only stared at her, looking about as betrayed as she'd ever seen him look. Laughing harder, she went to the kitchen to get him a treat. "You're the reason I can't have any friends over — you know that, don't you? You're rude, and you can't stand anyone around me. Well, I guess you'll have to get used to the smell, little man. I believe your favorite person in the world is going to smell a great deal like a bigger kitty. It would serve you right if I were to pick her over you."

After he sulked for a few hours, he finally got up on the couch with her. But he didn't sit on her lap, nor did he look at her when she said his name. The stupid animal was acting just like all the men she knew. Snooty and out of joint because she'd been out having fun. Well, not fun, but not here with him either.

Setting her alarm after not being able to get her stupid cat to like her again, she went to sleep. Tomorrow was going to be a good day. She might even be able to have a conversation with Rowan again. Micky was smiling when she felt herself roll over into sleep.

~*~

The paperwork was filed. The buildings she'd put in the works for demolition were ready to be taken down, and her daughters were sleeping on the floor in front of her. If only Kylan were home so she could tell him about her day.

Not that he didn't know it already. She had been

in constant contact with him since he'd left her the day before yesterday. Also, one or more of his family would stop by on the pretense of seeing how she was doing and would end up playing with Olivia and Michelle. She didn't really mind. But they were all so transparent when it came to seeing her.

"Mom." She looked at Olivia and smiled. "What do you suppose will happen to us once Michelle is working? I mean, we will have been with her for a very long time by then. Do you think she'll toss us away like old shoes?"

"I don't think she will, especially since I've seen the state of your old shoes. Why don't you just toss those out? I'll get you new ones." Olivia just stared at her, like she wasn't in the mood for jokes. "Are you worried about that, or hoping she'll give you some kind of part in her kingdom? Are you doing this for a reward, or because you want to? Those are things you need to ask yourself, honey."

"At first I was thinking I'd be her right-hand man. She'd need me with her during the entire process of being queen. You know, like I would know everything she was doing and be a part of it. That was what I thought for about ten seconds. Then I was thinking perhaps she'd just let me hang around with her. We'd still be sisters." Emmie asked Olivia what she thought now. Before she answered her, however, she looked down at the sleeping baby. "I think once she comes into her magic and is queen, we'll only be a distant thought of hers, and she won't ever visit us. That we will no longer be close, and I'll feel like I lost the very best friend I'll ever have."

"Oh, honey, you don't really think that, do you? That she'd forget you? My goodness. When you're not in the room with her now, she goes looking for you." She said it was because she didn't know anyone else that would get on the floor with her. "I don't think that's it at all. I think she genuinely loves you and loves being around you. While I don't have any sisters or brothers, I can't help but think the two of you will be closer than that."

"She'll be so powerful then. And I'll be this woman who at one time she slept with." When Olivia looked at her, Emmie felt her own eyes fill with tears. "I don't want her to grow up and leave me."

Holding Olivia while she cried, Emmie didn't say anything to her. She knew the thought of feeling like that. Knowing that someday no one would want you around. When her dad was getting sicker, it was how she'd felt. That he'd forget her soon. However, she knew this was different. Her dad would forget her simply because of his age and disease.

"When I was taking those classes online, do you remember that kid that used to come over to see you all the time? I don't remember his name." She told her. "That's it. Ronny. He was a nice sort of kid but annoying as hell. He would follow you around like a lost puppy. I swear there were times when I wanted to ask him if he'd bark on command. What happened to him?"

"He followed me around because I would feed him. It's not the same, Mom. Michelle is going to be queen. Ronny is going to be annoying all his life." She shook her head and pulled out her cell phone. Looking the boy up, she told Olivia how she'd seen this about him the other day. As Olivia read the article about him, she waited until she got to the very end. "He's invented something for lonely people that will be there for them. Mom, that thing looks just like me."

"I thought so too. However, he didn't quite get your eyes right. You see, he needed a friend, and for as much as he annoyed you, you were never mean to him. Never told him to go away. He used what you did for him to make himself a robot that will talk to him and keep him from being lonely all the time. It will be used for other people too. A companion. You were his." She asked her what that had to do with her and Michelle. "Plenty. You're showing her things that you love and like. Things that make you smile. She'll remember all these things too. Also, you've shown her something that no one but a sister can show her. How to be there for someone when they need you. She needs you. It's why she looks around for you when you run to the kitchen for a snack for the two of you. Or when the movie you're watching is over. Michelle is looking for you to introduce her to something else. Some other thing she doesn't know about. Honey, you're also showing her basic things that

Aurora never knew how to do. Share, for one thing. Not just food, but workload. You've shown Michelle how to pick out her clothes to wear for the day. How to pick out colors to color with. I know she scribbles right now, but I can tell when she's picking out colors to use. You've taught her the meaning of working on your education. How important it is to get things finished up in a timely manner rather than just playing all the time. Back to the shoes — you've taught her something very important. That she doesn't need to wear shoes in the house if she doesn't want to. That she needs a coat when she goes out. Sure, you know all these things like you've always known them. Who do you think taught you those things? I did. Grandpa did. Things that even as savvy and grown up as you are, you're teaching her that there is a place and a time for everything. Including wearing shoes."

When Michelle woke up, she reached for Emmie. It wasn't often that Michelle would reach for her when Olivia was in the room. But when she was on her lap, the baby patted her lap so Olivia would sit with her too. Emmie held the two of them like this until she realized they'd both fallen asleep in her arms. It was an amazing feeling to have someone trust you so much as to not have any trouble falling asleep while you were on guard.

Kylan came home just as the girls were waking up. They'd played in the snow today and were worn out, she told him, and that was why they were dozing again. Olivia went to Kylan first, hugging him and telling him how glad she was that he was home. Michelle, with her newfound way of getting around, crawled to her daddy and climbed up his leg so he'd pick her up. And as usual, when he left them, he'd come back bearing treats for all three of them and suggested that they go out to dinner. He said he wanted to show off his girls.

Neither of them mentioned the young woman he'd gone to save. Nor did he talk about the family over dinner. However, when they got home, and both of the girls were put to bed, he told her everything they'd done for her. Also how when he and Bryant had left, Rowan was sitting up in bed but still very weak.

"However, I'm betting in no time at all she'll be up and around. Her brother said she wasn't one to be idle. I can see that about her." She asked him if they'd found out any more about the shooting. Kylan shook his head and told her what he'd done. "Doctor Fleming had one of the bullets she'd not turned over to the police yet. I asked her if I could take it home with me to give to Fisher. He can touch things and figure out where they've been and who had them last. I stopped by there on the way home. He said he'd come by when he had something."

The two of them were headed to bed when Kylan paused on the stairs. She went back to him, sure it was bad news when he smiled at her. Wrapping his arm around her, then picking her up, he took her to their room while he told her what he'd just heard.

"Not only is Rowan awake, but demanding food. I

told the doctor she may well be hungry and to make sure she had plenty of fresh juices and fruit to eat and drink." Emmie asked him who had notified him. "Bryant. He left his number with her when we left. I did as well, but she said with having an infant in the house, she'd call me only if necessary. I did tell her we have the most amazing daughters in the world."

When she came out of the bathroom, Kylan still had his phone in his hand but was asleep. When she'd told him about the article she read about the Bronson family, he told her he'd read it. She smiled as she took the phone out of his hand and covered him up.

Slipping down the hallway to check on the girls, they were both asleep too. Emmie was headed back to her room when she realized it was only ten thirty. Going downstairs to work just a little bit more, she laughed at herself before she got halfway down the stairs.

Getting into bed with Kylan, she told herself she needed to be rested up for tomorrow. That she could work anytime. Closing her eyes, she felt her body relax in degrees and knew she was more tired than she'd thought. She was asleep in no time.

Whatever had woken her had her sitting up in bed. Emmie hadn't had any bad dreams in a long time and wondered what had dragged her from her sleep. Looking around the room, then reaching out beyond it, she touched lightly on her daughters to find them both asleep. Getting up, she looked out the window before going to see what had awakened her.

The man in the yard didn't scare her. She was afraid for him, however. He was in heavy clothing, or he was a large man, the fresh snow making him stand out brilliantly in the moonlight. Trying something she'd never done before, Emmie reached to his mind to see what was going on with him. He looked around as if he knew someone was touching his head, then he looked up at the window where she was.

He couldn't see her. Emmie was sure of that. Studying his face, she thought him to be kind of old but not as old as her dad. As he started walking around the yard again, she could almost see him talking to himself. Or another person. When someone touched her mind, she squeaked a little before remembering that no one could hear her up here either.

It's Nathan. The pack leader. She asked him if he saw the man in her yard. *I have — we have. We're not sure who he is, but he's not really doing anything to harm anyone. I was just about to run him off when he looked up at your windows. Is Kylan back?*

He is. I didn't wake him. Do you want me to? He said he'd like that, and she shook Kylan's arm to let him know someone was in the yard. Nathan spoke to him right away. "Are you going out there?"

"Yes. I think I might know who he is. If I ask you to stay up here, will you? I'm going to give the man some food." She just looked at him. "I did have to ask. He's an elderly gentleman that usually lives in town in one of the abandoned buildings. But there is a business in the one he likes to stay in."

"Mine?" He nodded as he pulled on his pants and socks. "Bring him in the house, Kylan, and I'll give him something he can take with him too. Also, he can sleep here if he wants."

"He won't. He'll say how nice it was of you to tell him he could, how you treated him like a real person, but he won't. I'll point out that he can stay in the barn, that it's warmer than the buildings that are left downtown."

She dressed herself and made her way to the kitchen. It was usually full of things like luncheon meats, but as soon as she entered, she saw their cook, Apple June there.

"I'm making him some soup in a big thermos I found." She was sure there hadn't been a thermos of any kind until she made it but didn't say anything. "Would you mind if I gave him some of those old blankets that were out in the barn before it was cleaned out? They're not doing us any good, don't you think?"

"I think that's a wonderful idea." As the two of them worked on getting him something to sleep in and food, Nathan and Kylan brought the man into the house. Emmie started to smile at the older man when she froze. She knew him. "What's your name? Please?"

"I knows you, miss. You're that little girl that was hurt powerfully by them people. The Landry ones." She nodded and had to sit down. "I heard tell you were here now. You marrying up one of the Prince men, you done all right with yourself. Are you all right?"

"I just never thought to see you again." He stepped closer to her, and she stood up. "You saved my life that day. Had you not helped me when that gun went off, I would have died."

Putting his fingers on the scar at her cheek, she let him. Tears rolled down both their cheeks as they just stared at each other. When he said he'd been wondering about her, she put her hand over his and asked him if he was all right.

"Right as rain. Right as rain. I got me a nice place here with your mister." She glanced at Kylan, then back at the man. "You sure did purty up, you did. Those men, they're dead too, ain't they?"

"Yes. I never knew your name. You—" She looked at Kylan and the others in the room with them. "I was shot by one of the bullets that killed the two of them in that basement. I thought I was going to die. The bullet went through the bottom of my chin and out of my cheek. I stumbled into this man's box, hiding from them. I didn't know they were dead by then."

"She was a mess then. Naked and bleeding. Her face beaten up so badly it was small wonder she only fell into my box that day." The man, his name still unknown to her, sat down at the table when the soup was given to him. "I used a little of what I am to stop the bleeding, then I fixed her up with a towel. Couldn't do much more for her. The police, they can be a might picky about stuff like that. Come on now, sit with me a spell."

All of them sat down to listen to the story she'd never told anyone else. Not the police. Not her dad. No one knew what this man had done for her. She reached for his other hand while he ate and spoke.

"I went back to find you but didn't know where you were. My eyes were swollen shut when I escaped, and I didn't know where I'd found you. Then you made it so I'd not be bleeding anymore from my face and opened one of my eyes. I was able to not just find my way to the police station but could see your face. You have no idea how many times over the years I looked for you." He laughed and told her he was here now. "You're not going to leave me again. I want you to stay here with me and my family."

"You're a good girl, but I can't no more sleep in a house than I can eat a steak anymore. No, I'll stay in your barn. That way, I can keep an eye on you and have me some quiet sleeping too." He looked at Kylan. "You're a good man, Kylan. A good one. You got yourself a fine wife here too."

"I know that."

After he was escorted to the barn, she sat in the kitchen, waiting on Kylan to return. He'd still not told her his name, and she was hoping he'd tell Kylan.

When he came back, all he did was shake his head.

"He said he's always wanted a good mystery to go with him. He said if he's around, he'll tell you tomorrow. I've known him for years, and I don't know it either."

After going to bed a second time, Emmie felt good. The man who had saved her was now safe too. Closing her eyes, sleep took her quickly and without any dreams.

Chapter 9

Kylan got up as soon as he knew it was close to sunrise. Dressing himself, feeling the urgency to get to the barn, he walked through the open door in time to see the man standing at the other end with the doors open already. Not bothering with niceties, he spoke to him, knowing everything there was to know about him.

"You step out into the sun, and I will tell her what a coward you are. Not only that but how you murdered your own wife." He told him he'd done no such thing. "Didn't you? Didn't you hire someone to change you both into what you are today without her permission? In fact, she told you she didn't want to live forever. That she wanted to die when she was supposed to, and not have to hang around after all her friends were gone."

"She had no friends I approved up." He turned toward him. "Don't you see what is going on here? Do you have any idea how much I've hated myself since that fateful day? You don't understand."

"Oh, I understand plenty. I know that you killed Mildred as if you'd shoved her into the sun with your own hands that morning. That instead of keeping all you'd acquired, you lost it all while you lay slumbering in rest after being changed. Your children, they were not nearly as — what did you call it? — special as you thought them to be. Both of them are dead too, aren't they?" Nodding, he stood in the open door but wasn't stepping out into the sun. "I won't give her that letter either. You don't deserve her forgiveness any more than you do from your own family. You, sir, have become just the sort of nightwalker everyone fears. A monster."

"I didn't know what they were when I left them there. I hadn't any idea that — " Kylan told him not to lie to him again. "I knew then. Are you happy to hear that? But I thought they'd change somehow. With us to scare them, they'd give up their ways."

"However, you never got around to it, did you? You just went around to everyone you knew, stealing from them and having a good time. Then you found yourself living in a box, afraid that someone would find you while resting and you'd die. Then my wife came along." He nodded, no longer looking outside the door. The sun had crested now, so it was up to him if he wanted to stand there and listen to his crimes. "Did you know who had raped her when you saved her life?"

"No. Not until a bit later. I mean, when she joined

me in the box, I thought I'd been given a nice little tasty treat. When I saw that she was bleeding, all I could think about was that my meal was going to die before I could have at her. She was naked, you know." Kylan said nothing. "Well, just as I was ready to take her throat out anyway, I smelled her. It was them. My son and grandson."

Kylan knew the story because when Emmie had had another bad dream, he'd held her. Each image had come to him as she saw them. But it was after she'd gone to sleep that he touched the mind of the man in the barn.

"You didn't just happen upon her tonight, did you? You came here to see if she'd figured out that not only were you related to the two men, but you were going to kill her anyway." Again he nodded. "Answer me, you bastard. Say it."

"I was going to kill her as soon as I found her. It's not like she has done anything with her life. What sort of person becomes an attorney and a truck driver? And that father of hers. He should have been put down when he first started being a burden. I was thinking of taking her for a few days, having some fun, then killing her. Just like them other two had started."

Kylan wanted to kill him. To shift into his tiger and tear him apart. But there was more that he was going to discuss with the man. To tell him about the girl he so eagerly wanted to kill. Leaning against the door on his side, he calmed his beast, the tiger within, while he thought of what he was going to say next.

"She had a child. Your great-granddaughter." That got his attention, but Kylan couldn't tell if it was good or bad. Reaching into his head, he could see that he didn't believe him. "Her name is Olivia. She had her at fourteen. Olivia is now the same age her mother was when she gave birth to her. All alone, except for the father you so willingly would have taken from her too."

"You lie." Pushing his memories of Olivia into the man's head, he watched as he staggered, then fell to the floor. Blood seeped from his eyes. "She's beautiful. Simply beautiful."

"Yes. She is." The back door opened, and he knew who had joined him. Since she didn't show herself, he didn't bother speaking to Olivia just yet. "Not only is she the most beautiful creature I've ever seen next to her mother, but she's brilliant. Also, not one you'd want to fuck with, as she's more powerful than you would ever hope to be."

"I want to see her." Kylan said it wasn't up to him. "Yes, it is, you moron. She'll do what you tell her. You bring her out here so I can see her. She's my great-granddaughter, damn it."

"I doubt very much she'd want to be anything to you when she finds out what else I know about you. You're the monster that I've called you. The man who not only fathered her grandda, who kidnapped her, but was grandfather to the man who turned out to be her father. The child molesters, all of you, who should have been killed long ago when you started to have your way with children." He told him he didn't do that anymore. "It wasn't for lack of trying, was it, Herbert Landry? You can no longer get to them. Children are much smarter than they used to be. Savvy about old men trying to lure them into their homes. Tell me, Herbert, how does it feel to know that had you killed Emmie, you would have ended the life of her child? Does that make you feel like a big man? Like someone that should be allowed to roam the streets at night?"

He could sense Olivia's anger, no longer confused as to why he was there, but understanding dawning on her quicker than it had him. When Emmie joined her little girl, he knew Olivia had called to her. It was time to get the man's true story out where they could hear his confession. Before he could ask him something, however, Herbert started talking.

"My Mildred knew what sort of monsters we was. She called the police on me so many times it's a wonder they didn't take her more serious." He looked at him. "I had hoped when I had us changed, she'd be a little easier to live with. But damned if she didn't just go on out and meet the sun, just days after she heard that her boy had been killed and what he'd been up to when it happened."

"Yes, I can well imagine she had it in her head that you'd kill your son and his offspring when they started taking up where you left off. But you did nothing, as you had your entire human life. You killed them all—you know that, don't you? Your son, grandson, and wife. Just because you thought you knew so much more than they did. And since the police never caught on that you were taking children and molesting them, that made it all right." Kylan laughed bitterly. "I'm so glad you knew nothing of Olivia. There is no telling what that child might have had to endure while you were hanging around her all the time. Knowing you, you might well have done to her what your son did to my wife. You deserve nothing from them."

"Damn you. I want you to tell her to get her ass out here. I have a right to know my own great-grandchild." Olivia, with her mom, came from the corner of the barn and stared at the man. "Come closer, please? I want to have a good look at you. From here, you're the spitting image of my dear wife."

"Who I'm betting I would have liked a great deal more than I do you. You're nothing to me." Olivia looked at her mother and then at Kylan before staring at Herbert. "I wouldn't come any closer to you even if you were chained up like the animal you are."

"You have no right to say things like that to me. Why, if I was closer to you, I'd surely beat your ass for that." She moved, not that he saw her moving, but Olivia was suddenly in front of Herbert with him lifted up off the ground. "What the hell are you doing to me? Let me go this minute. Damn it, Kylan, let me go."

"I'm not touching you. Nor am I the one holding you there. That would be my daughter." Putting his arm around Emmie, he pulled her closer to him, needing not just her touch but her scent to calm him. "I told you, did I not, that she was stronger than you? Whatever she does to you right now is less than you deserve. Christ, to think at one time I felt sorry for you."

"I'm your great-granddaddy, child. Doesn't that mean anything to you? We could get to know each other. I can teach you a few — " Herbert didn't just stop talking, but his mouth disappeared. Emmie walked to her daughter, putting her hands on her shoulders.

"Without him, I'd not have you. Without his so-called help, I wouldn't have lived to have you and Michelle. Met and fallen in love with the Prince family. Fallen in love and married the greatest man I know. You'd not have the best dad there is in the world in Kylan. Without him, the start of this all, there would be no one to care for your sister." She asked her what she wanted her to do. "I'm not going to tell you what to do with him. However, if you're planning to kill him, which is what I'd do, then I'd make it quick. As we heard, he's a monster and doesn't deserve to live. It's how he dies that will matter to you more than anything you have to think about in the future. Understand?"

"Yes, you mean what can I live with after he's dead and gone." Emmie told her that was right. "Can I live with him having a quick death? Or do I want him to suffer in the same ways you have since his family came into your life?"

"All the suffering disappeared the moment they laid you in my arms. All the bad things that happened to me, they went away when you looked into my eyes. Whatever pain had been put on me, it wasn't an issue any longer the first time you called me mom." Olivia asked her if that was true. "Yes. It wasn't until this very moment, however, that I realized it. The moment you decided to avenge me. Don't do this for me, Olivia. He was dead before he found us, and you killing him now will be no different. Kill him in a way you can live with."

"I'll do it." Kylan walked up to the two of them, his family. Wrapping them up in his arms, he told them again that he'd kill the monster. "He means less than anything to me. Less than he does to the two of you. I will end his life before he can hurt anyone else. It would be my pleasure to do this for the two women in my life that mean more to me than my own life."

Before any of them could come to a decision on how the man would be taken away, Kylan's entire family, as tigers, stood in the doorway where Herbert had been. They must have spoken to Olivia, told her they'd take care that he never bothered them again. As soon as the fur on the backs of their necks stood up, Dad jumped up at Herbert, tearing his left leg off and dragging it away.

Herbert dropped to the ground then. Olivia turned her face toward Kylan's chest, and he held her and her mother that way. As one at a time, his brothers and father tore the man apart, he knew for so long as he had lived, he'd never seen them kill like they did the monster that had tormented so many. As each part they tore off was carried away, he did wonder for a moment where they were taking them.

He knew they'd not eat him. First of all, they never did that for food anymore. Secondly, he was a vampire, and that would be poison to their systems for some time. It wouldn't kill them, but they'd be sick. When there was nothing left but ash from the sun hitting the blood, he knew the body parts had suffered the same fate. There'd be no more than a pile of dust to show that he'd ever been around.

Going into the house when it was over, he sat them both down on the couch and went to get Michelle. Taking her to the women in his life, he simply handed her to them, and she seemed to know they needed cuddling. Mother and daughter loved on the child, and she loved them back.

Olivia called out to us. She told us what was happening and asked that one of us would come and rescue you. I think she was afraid you'd not take it well, killing a man. To be honest with you, Kylan, it was difficult for any of us to decide who would do it for her. So, in the end, we all did. It was one of the best pleasures I've had in slaying someone like that. He told Bryant what they were doing now. *Good for them. And for you. I think all of you needed this ending.*

I didn't know when I invited him to live in our empty buildings all those years ago. I had no idea to even touch him, to find out of he was killing people. I was a sap. Bryant told him he'd seen him around too and hadn't done anything either. *Do you suppose he did that to us? Made us trust him? Even if you don't think he did, I could live with that better than thinking he took me for a fucking ride.*

I'm not sure, but you're more than likely right. Honestly. They both laughed a little. *I'm going to get in touch with his maker if he's still around. He'll have to be punished for the crimes against the wife. Someone needs to pay for her being changed against her will.*

I hope he gets what he deserves too.

When Bryant didn't say anything, Kylan laid back on the couch. He was suddenly exhausted, his body just beginning to realize how long he'd been awake.

His brother spoke to him again. What he said, he didn't know. Not able to fight the way his body was shutting down, he knew if it was really important, someone here would shake him awake. At least he hoped so.

~*~

Benjamin hated waiting until the time he'd been told to be at the house. There was something going on, and he wanted answers, not time on his hands. Looking at his pocket watch, a holdover from his time as a human, he slipped it back in his pocket when he saw that no more than a minute had passed since he looked before.

"You're very impatient." He turned to look at a woman he'd not seen in centuries. Bowing down before her, he stood when Aurora told him to stand before she hit him. Again. "You're going to see them then? To talk to the family that has suffered."

"I'm not the maker." She said she knew that. "I thought them all dead, to be frank with you, my lady. When I found out that Peter was making anyone who asked into a version of himself, I ended their lives as they wanted. I had no idea he'd made this couple vampires too. The wife, she suffered badly by him."

"No more so than the child when she was caught by them. Did you know that people thought her a hero? Right up until the time they found out she carried a child. Then they wanted nothing to do with her. Some even went so far as to take back the medal of honor they pinned on her while she was in the hospital." Benjamin said he'd not known. "Nor did you try to find out, did you?"

"No. I was neglect in my duties as a vampire. I will tell you, my lady, I would have ended their lives as soon as I knew. All of them. I might be a monster of the night, but I do not condone taking and hurting small children." She asked him to have a seat. It was only then that he figured out she'd moved them to her estate. The bright light of the day didn't bother him here. However, he was almost afraid to get too comfortable. Aurora, the queen of faeries, was the most powerful being he'd ever encountered.

"Why have you not become my friend, Benjamin? Why have we gone this long and not at least had tea together? Talked about your role in the world?" He told her that, quite frankly, he was afraid of her. "As you should be. As well as the child Olivia. She will be my second in command soon enough. I have already formed an army with her family. You'd not want to fuck with me."

She was pouring tea from a lovely teapot into equally beautiful cups. The fragrance was something floral, like roses, he thought. Aurora had said he'd not want to fuck with her as if she were asking him how many lumps of sugar he wanted in his tea. With trembling hands, he took the cup when it was offered and waited on her to drink first. That was the way he'd been taught from the time he was a very young man. Never do anything before the queen in the room.

"Do you think I should kill you? I had it in my mind to do so when I heard of what happened today." He told her he was profoundly sorry. "Yet that doesn't seem like enough to me. I'm sure it won't to Olivia and her family. What are you going to do for them? Remember, too, that I know of all your misdeeds, Benjamin. Just as I know of those you've made."

"Money?" Aurora said she didn't need it. Nor magic, if that was what he was going to say. "Then I don't know. I have nothing left to offer her."

"You do. And to think I thought that would have been the first thing you offered for her. My goodness, have you become selfish in your old age?" His castle. He had a castle almost as beautiful as the one he was in now. Surely she couldn't think that he'd — "Yes, I do think that is what you should offer her. I mean, she did have to do your dirty work for you. Her mother suffered needlessly because of you. Benjamin, think of the things she could do to you. If you have trouble with that, let me help you."

The pain behind his eyes was excruciating. But it was the images that hurt him more. The ways he was to suffer. Not die. Nay, she'd not allow him to die before she got what she wanted from him. While he had no idea why he was to suffer so badly, it mattered little. His children had hurt her.

"What will a child do with a castle?" Another round of images flashed, these no less painful to his head, but better in that he wasn't being taken apart by her. "Make it a summer home? Are you mad? What kind of idiot do you take me for?"

His words spilled from his mouth before he could stop them. Even as he was being ripped apart on the inside, he knew she'd not kill him either but would make the suffering he was to endure from Olivia like child's play. He begged her to stop. When she did, he was in no less pain, but at least he knew he'd heal from this. For now.

"I will turn it over to her immediately." She asked

him what he would do for the tigers. "What tigers? I have had nothing to do with your precious tigers since you warned me away. Do you think to make me a pauper? Someone without the simple things, such as a place to rest or money to buy myself a nice place to live now that you've taken my home away?"

"I took nothing." The heat that accompanied her words burnt at his face and hands. The teacup, so delicate in his hands, shattered as he tried to hold onto himself. When she seemed to gather herself up, her anger gone for the moment, she handed him another cup and leaned back in her chair. "I took nothing from you, Benjamin. It is what you owed them that you need to give over. Nothing you have will make up for what was done to her mother, but since there was a child born, one that I've taken into my heart, I will allow you to live for another day. However, there is the matter of my tigers. They destroyed the monster you allowed to be created. Even if what you say to me is true—which, I don't believe you did try to find them all…you let the biggest monster slip by—do you know how many children he killed before I was able to keep them away from him? Thousands, if you want the truth."

There was nothing he could say. She was right. He hadn't done nearly enough to keep the world safe from the monster that had been made. Looking at her, he was sure this side of the queen was one that few saw or even encountered because they'd pissed her off.

"You don't want to see me angry, Benjamin. You might think you have, but you'd be wrong. I am. Angry, I mean. But I know you're going to do the right thing and make sure my family is taken care of." He knew better than to argue with her now. Whatever she wanted, he'd give her. As the mother of faeries, she'd be one to kill him without a second thought. "What are you going to do for my tigers?"

"They will have all that I have." She nodded, and he knew it wasn't enough. Not yet. "I shall be at their beck and call, any time of the day or night. I will gladly be a slave to them."

"Good. Now that we've reached a good understanding of what you will do, you will go to the king of the tigers and tell him what it is you wish to do. Do not mention my name, Benjamin, or it will go badly for you."

He shivered at the face he saw there. No beauty in it. Nothing but pure anger. Whenever anyone thought of a monster, he knew they'd come nowhere close to thinking of the beautiful woman sitting before him. When she stood, so did he. The small faerie that came to sit upon his shoulder had him thinking she wasn't done with him just yet.

"This is Cart. He was once faerie to Olivia, but when she came into her power, he knew she was beyond what he could do for her. So he will be...how should I explain this? He will be with you forever. Watching over you. Taking care that you will do as you promise. Also, you should be aware I've taken the ability to meet the sun from you. I don't wish you to be able to have an out when they need you most." He did have a thought that she'd been planning this for some time now. That after putting all of it together, she knew just when to approach him.

Bowing before her once again, he found himself at the front door to the home he'd been waiting to enter — the house of the king of tigers. Benjamin wondered if the man knew of his title but decided he didn't want to know. Whatever Aurora had planned for him was between the two of them.

Knocking, he smiled a little. Benjamin would never play chess with the queen. Nor the young woman, Olivia. He knew of Kylan, his part in keeping his family safe. He knew all the Princes. However, he thought he didn't know half as much as there was to know. Not even close.

"You will behave, will you not, vampire?" He told Cart that he would. And that he'd not give him any trouble either. "You'd better not. These people are the only thing between life and death for you. It would be good for you to remember that."

"I shall. But I doubt you'll allow me to forget it, will you, Cart?" He said it was his job. "Thank you for being here with me. I know it's not your want in life to spend days with a vampire. But I thank you for it."

"Do not suck it up with me, sir." He corrected the

faerie. "Whatever the term is, do not do it to me. I am much smarter than you might think. While I don't think we'll be friends, we might just come to an understanding someday. Is that all right with you?"

"Very much so."

He was laughing a little when the door was opened. The man there, a butler he thought him to be, said he'd get the master of the house. Benjamin thought he'd like to start off on a good footing here. To do what he was told to do, but also make the king feel as if he could really depend on him. Benjamin thought perhaps he might enjoy having a friend or two for a time. He saw the big tiger coming toward him with his wife, the two of them looking like well-bred humans with a great deal of money.

Benjamin smiled at them. "You don't need to invite me in. If you'd like, we can talk here."

"Come in. You're invited to come in and have a conversation with us for just today." So he'd been told about that little trick, had he? Good. Trust was something he'd have to earn from them. "Benjamin, I'm afraid I have some news for you. Concerning a child of yours."

"Yes, I felt his death. Herbert Landry. I have been negligent in keeping an eye on him. I'm also to understand he has caused more than a little trouble for you and your family. I will make restitution on both his behalf and mine." He could tell the man was confused by his readiness to take care of things. Good. He wanted to be one up on someone today. "I know you've no need for it, but you shall have all his funds given to your family to be used as you see fit. I'm afraid there isn't nearly as much as I'd like, so for my part of his idiocy, I'm giving over my entire estate for the deeds his family forced upon one of yours as well."

He didn't know what the tiger was going to say, but his wife put her hand on his and smiled at him. "That would be good. What else will you be handing over for what trouble he's caused? You should know that there is a child from his children. One that was conceived by rape. A brutal one too. I should think something more should be set aside for her."

He thought about what he'd told Aurora. Being around for them should they need it. He didn't know that the child was conceived in rape, a brutal one at that. He might have been told but had forgotten about it. Getting down on his knees, he asked her what she'd want of him. Even, he told her, if it was his life. He'd gladly give it to her.

"I don't think there needs to be any more deaths because of this, do you?" He didn't answer. As he told her, anything she wanted. "There is a man, his name is Collier, father to the woman they hurt. You can help him. Give him a clear mind so he can live his life with his child and grandchildren. You can do that, can't you? If you cannot, please tell me now."

"He has dementia? The issue lies with his brain?"

She said it did. "I can help him have a clear mind, yes. But you need to understand, he might lose a great deal of his memories. To take him back to the time when he was only a little bit harmed by it would mean a great many memories would need to be remade for him."

"I have spoken to his daughter, the one that has cared for him for so long, and she said she would just have to fill in his blanks with newer memories. Ones that he could smile and laugh about now." Benjamin sat back on his heels and looked at the beautiful woman before him. "Also, I would very much like it if you were to become a part of our family. Someone we can trust. Someone we can call on as a friend. Do you think that would be something else you'd like to do with us?"

"Why?" She asked him what he meant. "Why are you doing this? You know I'm a vampire. That I made the very person that has harmed so many of your family members. Why would you like me, of all people, to become a friend of the family? I don't understand."

"Perhaps I can explain." The woman that entered the room startled him. He knew Kylan's wife was a beauty, but this woman, even in her first stages of having a child, seemed to glow. "My father means the world to me. I've lost a bit of him over the years that I thought I'd never see again. If you do this for me, for us, then I should like for you to be someone that would be around, to remind us how fragile life can be. Someone that even my father would know he could call friend too."

Benjamin didn't know what to say.

The child that was with her, Olivia, he'd bet, came to sit on the floor in front of him. She looked deep into him, reaching a place that once held his heart that had long since died. Or so he thought. When she smiled at him, he couldn't help it, he smiled back at her.

"You've been hurt too, haven't you?" He nodded. "Someone changed you without your permission when it wasn't thought of to be a crime. You have lived your life in anger for so long you didn't care what happened to you."

"Yes." He didn't ask her how she knew this. But he was sure she knew even more about him than he remembered. "You're very powerful. But along with that, you're very beautiful as well. I think I should like to be your friend."

"I would as well." Putting out her hand, he took it before he could think he should caution himself on what might happen between them with the exchange. The tingle in the region where his heart had long since stopped beating made him think he was more alive right now than he'd been when he was human. "Thank you, Olivia Prince. I will help your grandda, with your help."

"Deal."

The rest of the afternoon was all of them sitting around talking. He even enjoyed a scone, something he'd not had in centuries. While he wasn't older than the tigers, he was old. Food had come to mean less to him than friendship. Or so he'd thought.

Benjamin was happy when he left the home. Happy to do as they wanted. He thought perhaps that he'd still be at their beck and call, though he would enjoy it a great deal more now.

Chapter 10

Micky and Rowan loaded up the car with the few things they planned to take with them. Mostly it was snacks and bottled water and juice, but it was a road trip they both wanted. Maybe even needed a little.

"I can't believe how quickly my house sold." She told Rowan she thought she'd gotten a good deal on it too. "Yes, I did. Now I have to figure out what I'm going to do when I get back. Taking a leave from the station house wasn't my idea, but now that I'm going with you, I think I might enjoy it. Are you sure you don't mind taking me with you?"

"It'll be just what we both need." Not only had her sister sold her house, but she'd gotten someone to take over the running of the nursing home. "We neither one have ties to hold us back or that we have to rush back to. Roone and the others are going to come to see us when they can. This will be better than the cruise we were going to take."

"I still want to take that cruise with you." Micky wanted that too, but now wasn't so sure she'd be able to enjoy it. "Are you going to tell me what is going on, or are you going to make me guess? Tell me."

"I have cancer. It's in my lungs, lymph nodes, as well as my breasts. It's not that I've not had checks every year, but this is an aggressive form that is going to take my life. I don't want to die, Rowan." She said she didn't want her to either and hugged her. "I wanted this to be so much fun for us. The two of us getting out and seeing things we might not have otherwise."

"You're not going to die." She nodded at her. "No. You're not. We're going to make our first trip out to see the family that saved me. If they can put me back together the way they did, you won't be a problem."

"I can't ask them to do that. They saved you. That was more than enough." Rowan told her she'd tell them, not ask, and that saving her without her bestie wasn't good enough. "This is why I didn't want to tell you. I knew you'd want that too."

"I can't go on without you, Micky. You're as much my twin as Roone is. I need you." She said she needed her too. "Do they know? Any of them?"

"Mark does. The doctor I usually used was out of town when I fell. It wasn't that big of a deal, but Mark saw me in the emergency room and found out. Told me about it too." She told her it would be all right. "No. This is all we're going to do. Go on this trip, have some fun before I'm too weak to go on, then I'll die peacefully in my sleep with you holding my hand."

Getting into the car, she hoped that would be the end of it. However, she should have known better. Rowan was not one to put off. The first hundred miles or so was her talking about how they were going to approach the family. To beg, if they needed to, for what they wanted them to do for them.

By the time Rowan let it go, they were outside the city limits of the town the Prince family was from. At some point, Rowan had driven them right there. Micky's nap was the perfect time for her to get off the highway and to the city. She shouldn't have told her.

"Because they shared their blood with me, I'm betting I have some sort of beacon I can contact them with. What is it they do in those dirty books you read?" She told her they weren't dirty, but romance. "Potato, potahto. Whatever. What do they do?"

"They sort of mind reach out for them. I doubt that would work anyway. I mean, it's only in books. Right?" Rowan turned and smiled at her. "You did it, didn't you? Have you no shame?"

"Not where you're concerned, no, I don't. We've been invited for dinner. I'm talking to Bryant right now. He thinks it's funny that we're here. They were all just talking about me." Misty said they should find a hotel. "Nope, we're staying with them. They have plenty of room, and we're going there."

The drive through town was slow going, but it was a nice little town. The more they got out of what could only be considered downtown area, the houses got bigger and pricier. Rowan pulled into the drive of one of the biggest houses she'd ever seen. She asked her if this was right.

"You tell me. Is that him on the front porch?" Not only was it Bryant, but he was waving at them. The woman with him could only be Harper, the woman she'd spoken to briefly when she'd called to talk to her husband. "I'm assuming that's a yes. Come on, dork. We're going to have a lovely dinner with them, then we're going to see about saving you for me. This might not work the way I want it to, but I've got my gun. We'll just have to make them help you."

Before she could tell her she was insane, which she was sure Rowan was, she was in the car all alone. Getting out, she had a moment when she was dizzy and didn't let go of the door just yet. When a tiger came to the car beside her, she wondered if this would be an easier way to die than the cancer she had.

"Hello." She smiled at the man who walked from the porch to her. "I'm Collier. Emmie is my daughter. Kylan is her husband. He wants me to talk to you. Can I do that for you? Also, you should know that this is Marcus."

"Is he planning on having me for dinner? I'm ill.

He should know that too." Collier told her she had been ill. "I'm sorry. No one has touched me here. I can't be cured."

"He said you were touched by your sister. Hugged, too, if he doesn't miss his bet. Marcus said you were cured of the cancer the moment she held you in her arms. However, he is very happy you've come to visit them." She said she didn't understand. "Marcus said they explained to you about the magic they used on your sister. Also, telling you they didn't know how it would work with her. She can apparently heal people with just a touch. Even the cut on your leg you did this morning while shaving is gone. He said you missed a spot on your ankle."

"Does he have any manners at all?" Collier laughed and said all of them did, usually. She looked at where she'd cut herself badly this morning and found that not only was it gone, but there wasn't a scar. "I don't understand this. We came here...Rowan has a gun. She planned on using it on your family if they didn't help me."

"Not that it matters, but since you're healed, we don't have to worry about that." She asked him why it didn't matter. "We're all immortal, including you and your sister. Are you coming in for dinner? I'm starved."

When he walked away, she looked at the tiger. He was staring at her like her cat did, who she had left in the back of the car. Going to get it out of the cage, she warned the big tiger that she wasn't too keen on bigger cats. As soon as she leapt from her hands, the cat was gone.

"Micky? Are you coming in or staying out there all day?" She looked at her sister, then at the tiger. "Come on. We're all waiting on you?"

"Something is going on here, isn't it?" He nodded at her. "Do you suppose we're going to be unhappy with whatever it is?" The cat shrugged like a human would. Then he took off for the side of the house. "I've entered *The Twilight Zone*. I just know it. I'm going to start hearing that scary music, then end up in some cornfield where I'll never be heard from again."

Going into the house, she felt calmed. The aroma coming from the dining room had her following her nose. Whatever they were serving, she wanted some of it. Sitting down next to her sister, she started piling up her plate. The tiger, in the form of a man, came in and sat down too. This was just going to drive her over the edge, she knew it.

AWARD WINNING, BESTSELLING AUTHOR

Kathi Barton, a winner of the Pinnacle Book Achievement award as well as a best-selling author on Amazon and All Romance books, lives in Nashport, Ohio, with her husband, Paul. When not creating new worlds and romance, Kathi and her husband enjoy camping and going to auctions. She can also be seen at county fairs with her husband, who is an artist and potter.

Her muse, a cross between Jimmy Stewart and Hugh Jackman, brings her stories to life for her readers in a way that has them coming back time and again for more. Her favorite genre is paranormal romance, with a great deal of spice. You can visit Kathi on line and drop her an email if you'd like. She loves hearing from her fans. aaronskiss@gmail.com.

Follow Kathi on her blog: http://kathisbartonauthor. blogspot.com/

www.ingramcontent.com/pod-product-compliance
Lightning Source LLC
Chambersburg PA
CBHW020619180626
46810CB00007B/2853